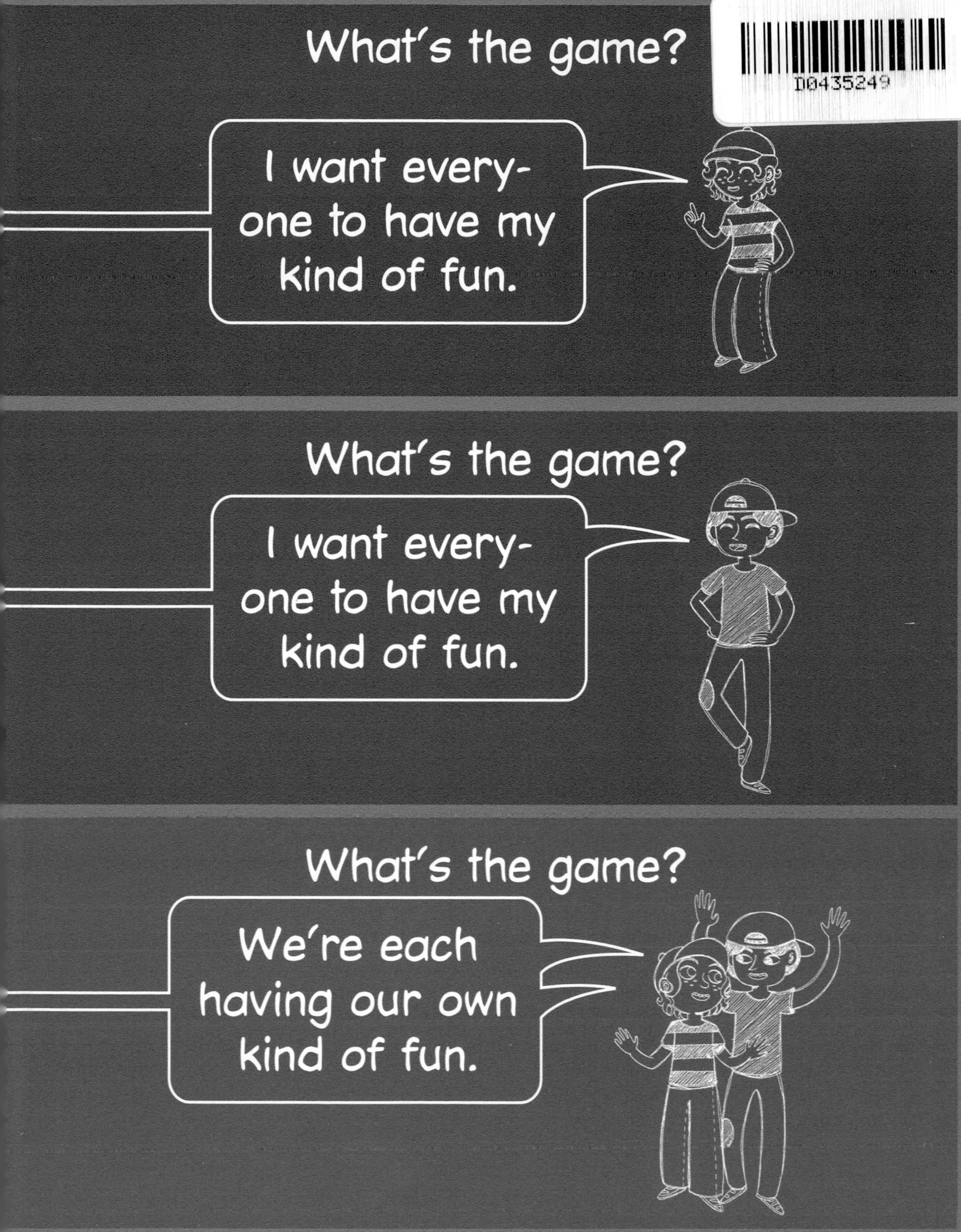
What's the game?
I want every-one to have my kind of fun.
What's the game?
I want every-one to have my kind of fun.
What's the game?
We're each having our own kind of fun.

...and get the whole story.

A GRAPHIC NOVEL

LEE NORDLING & MERITXELL BOSCH

THREE
STORY
BOOKS

GRAPHIC UNIVERSE™ • MINNEAPOLIS

For Cheri, the love of all of my lives.
And a special thanks to Andrew Karre and Carol Hinz
for embracing this vision.
– Lee Nordling

This book is dedicated to Jan, my precious little boy.
Manuel, without your help I would not have finished the book.
And thanks to you, reader, to have this book in your hands.
– Meritxell Bosch

Lee Nordling is an Eisner Award nominee and
an award-winning writer, editor, creative director,
and book packager. He worked on staff at
Disney Publishing, DC Comics, and
Nickelodeon Magazine.

Meritxell Bosch is an Eisner Award nominee and
a graphic novel artist and writer, illustrator,
character designer, colorist, and art teacher,
living in Barcelona, Spain.

Story and script by Lee Nordling
Art by Meritxell Bosch

Copyright © 2015 by Lee Nordling & Meritxell Bosch

SheHeWe and Three-Story Books were placed,
designed, and produced by The Pack.

Graphic Universe™ is a trademark of Lerner
Publishing Group, Inc.

Graphic Universe™
A division of Lerner Publishing Group, Inc.
241 First Avenue North
Minneapolis, MN 55401 USA

For reading levels and more information, look up this
title at www.lernerbooks.com.

Library of Congress Cataloging-in-Publication Data

Nordling, Lee.
    SheHeWe / by Lee Nordling ; illustrated by
Meritxell Bosch.
      pages cm. – (Three-Story Books)
    Summary: "Tells the story of a boy and girl and
games they play, separately and together, through
clever wordless comics." –Provided by publisher.
    ISBN 978-1-4677-4574-1 (lib. bdg. : alk. paper)
    ISBN 978-1-4677-4578-9 (pbk.)
    ISBN 978-1-4677-4579-6 (EB pdf)
    [1. Graphic novels. 2. Games–Fiction. 3. Stories
without words.] I. Bosch, Meritxell, illustrator.
II. Title.
PZ7.7.N67Sh 2015
741.5'973–dc23   2014021929

Manufactured in the United States of America
1 – BP – 7/15/15

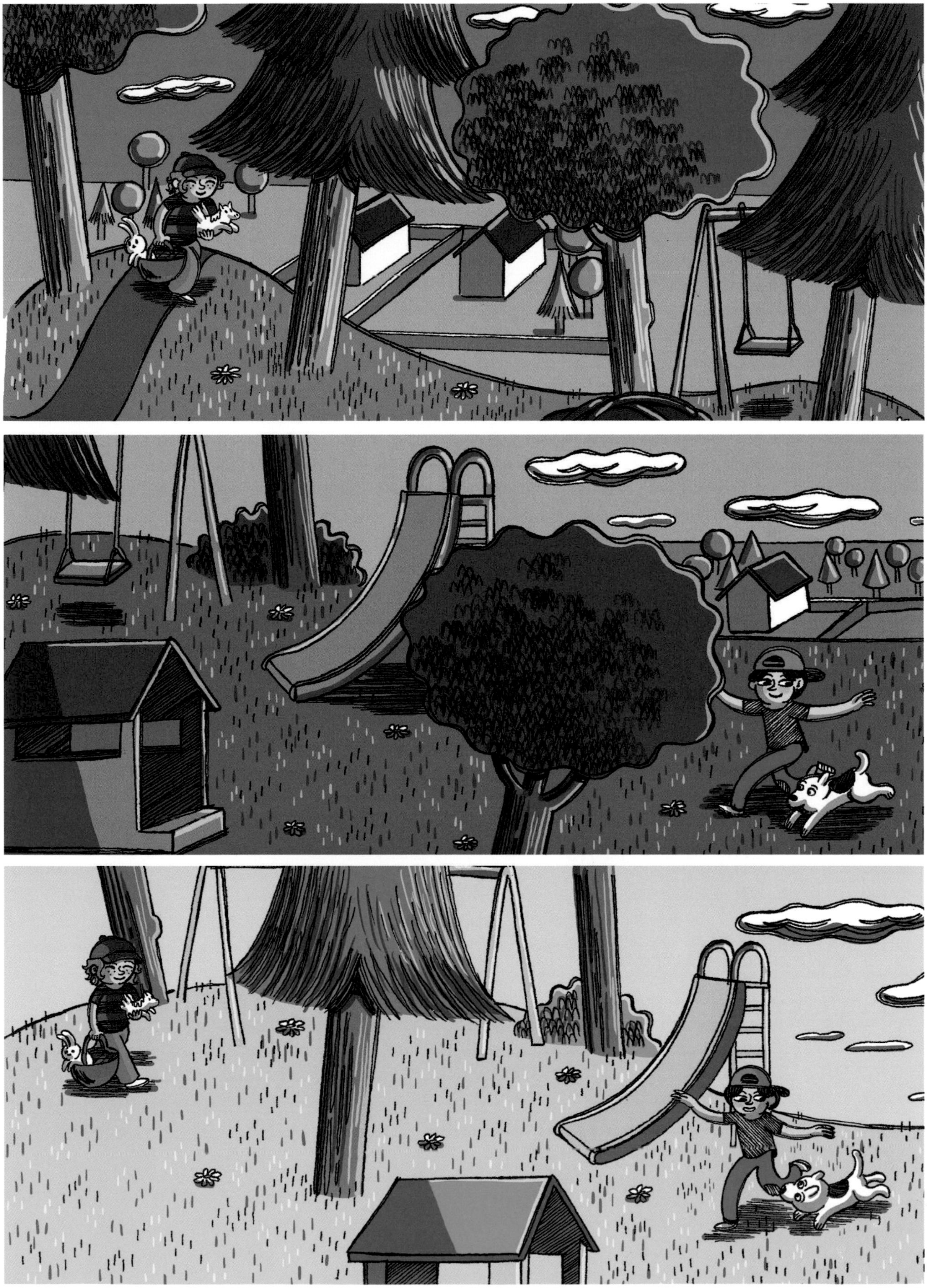

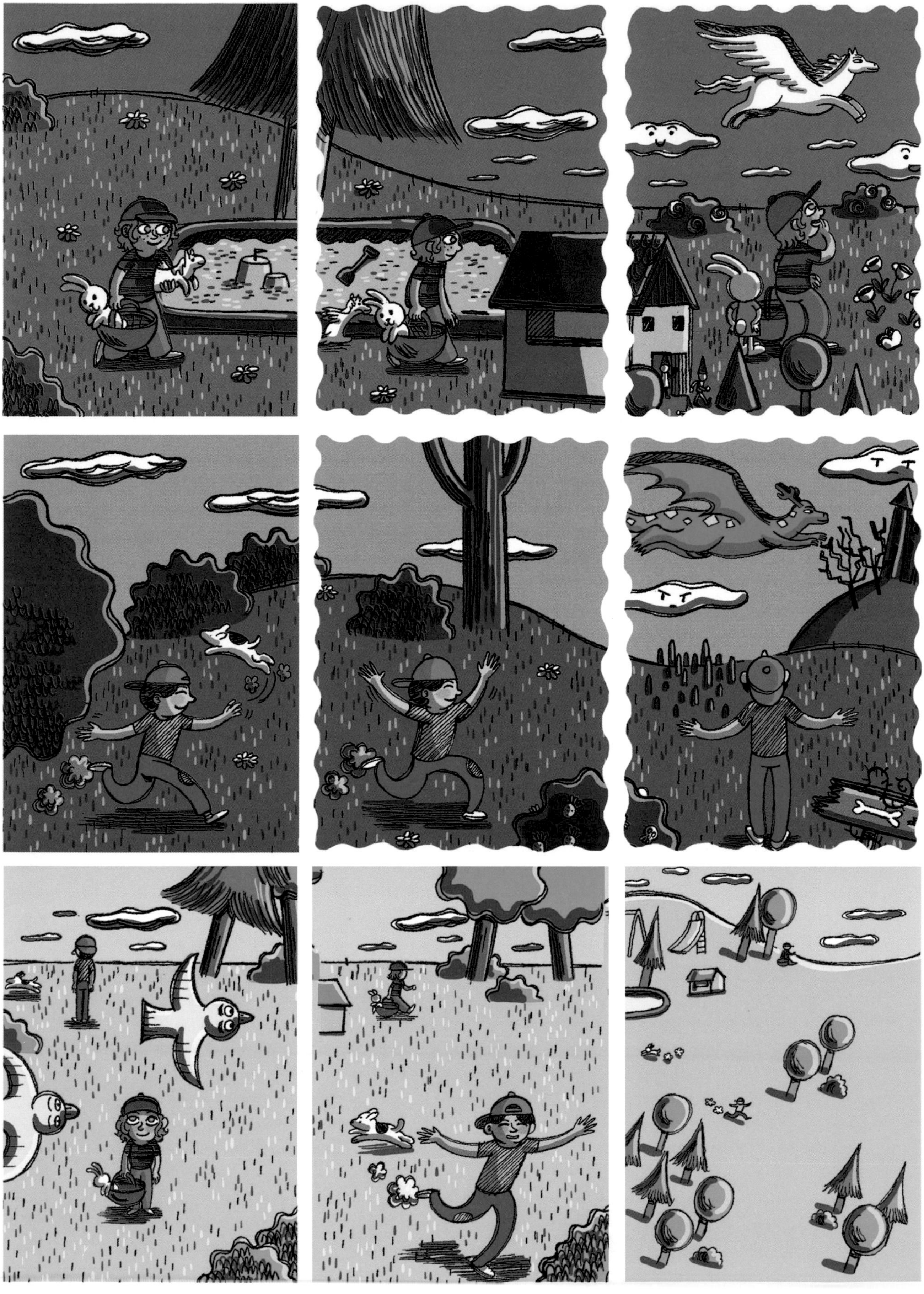

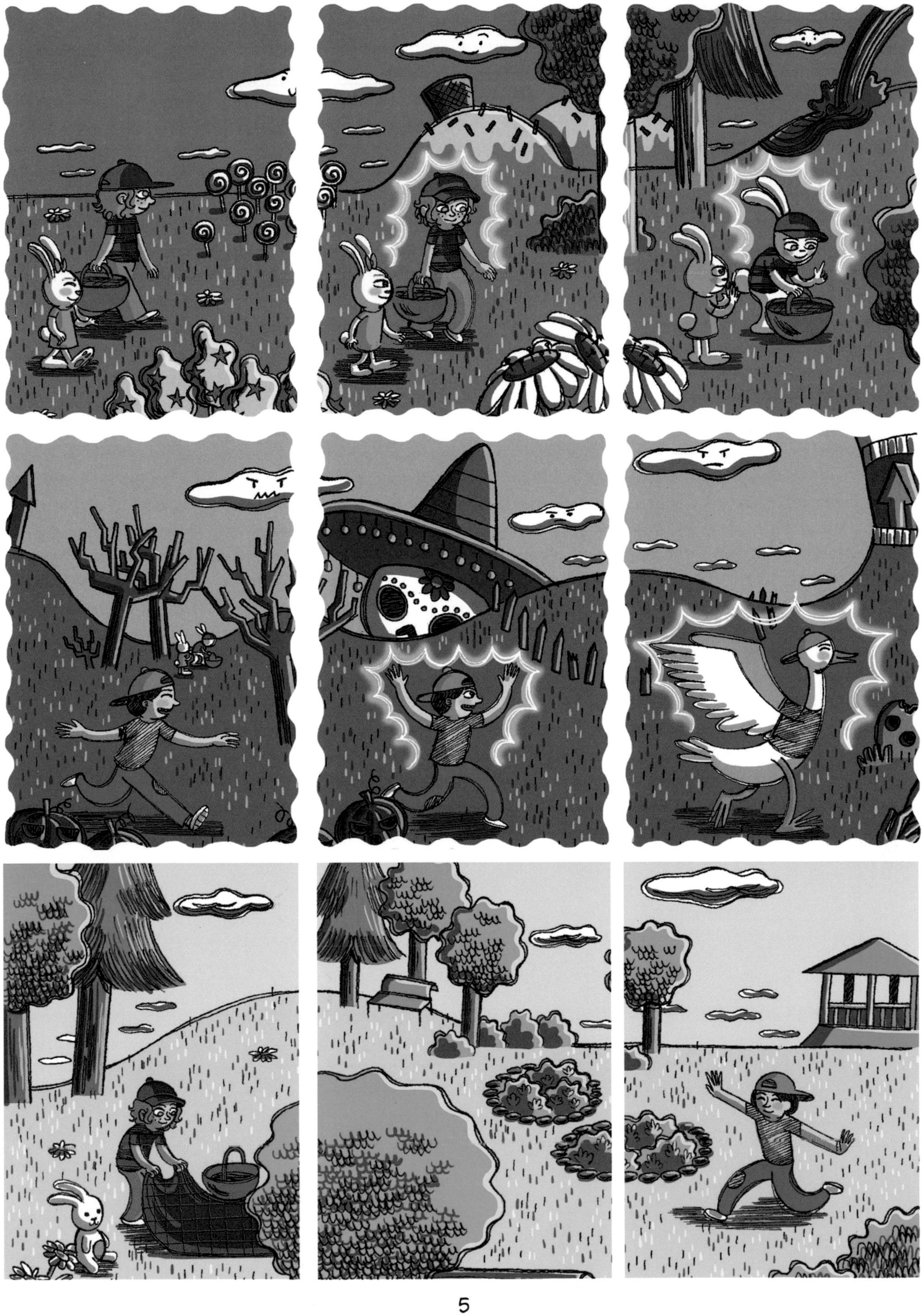

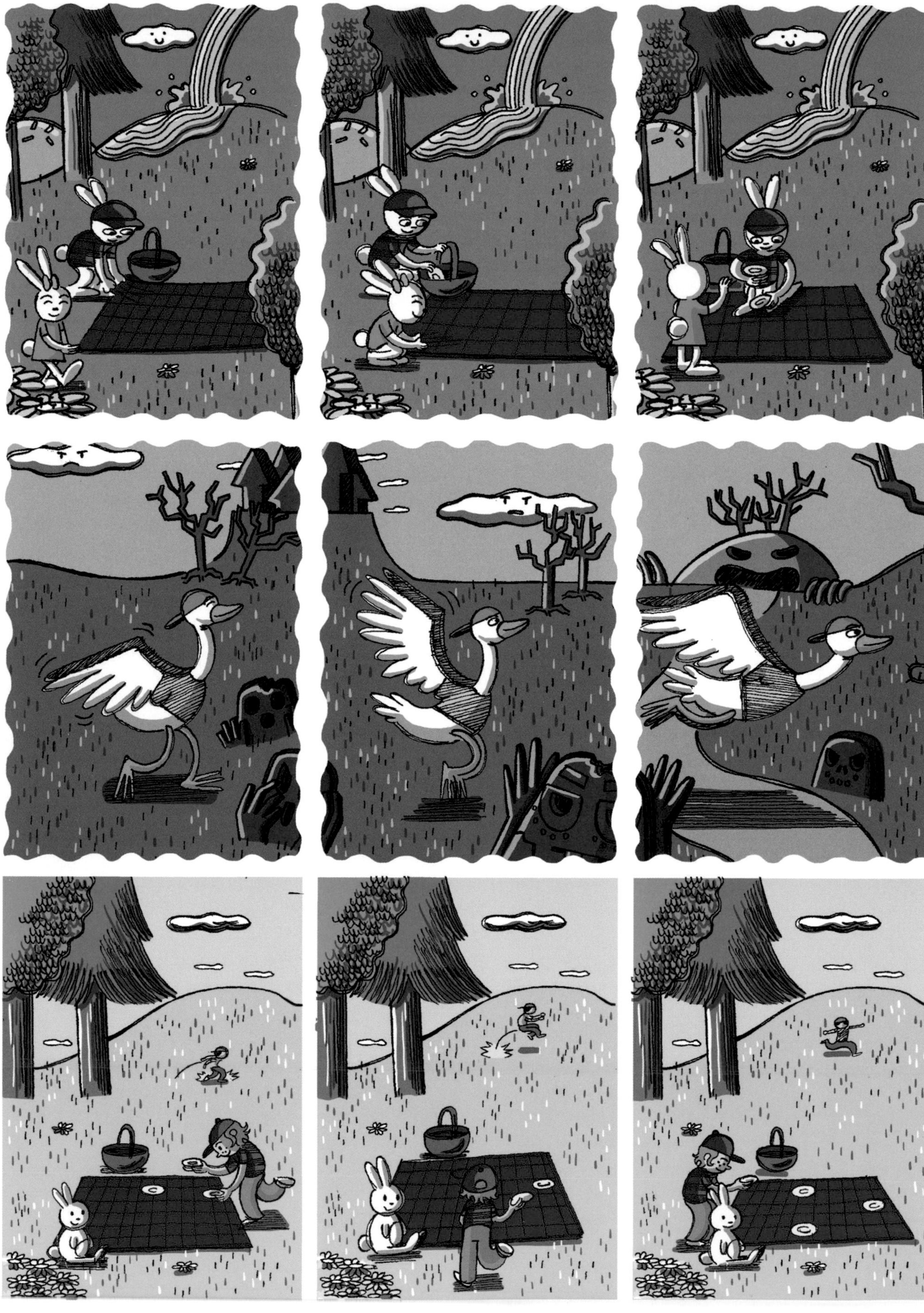

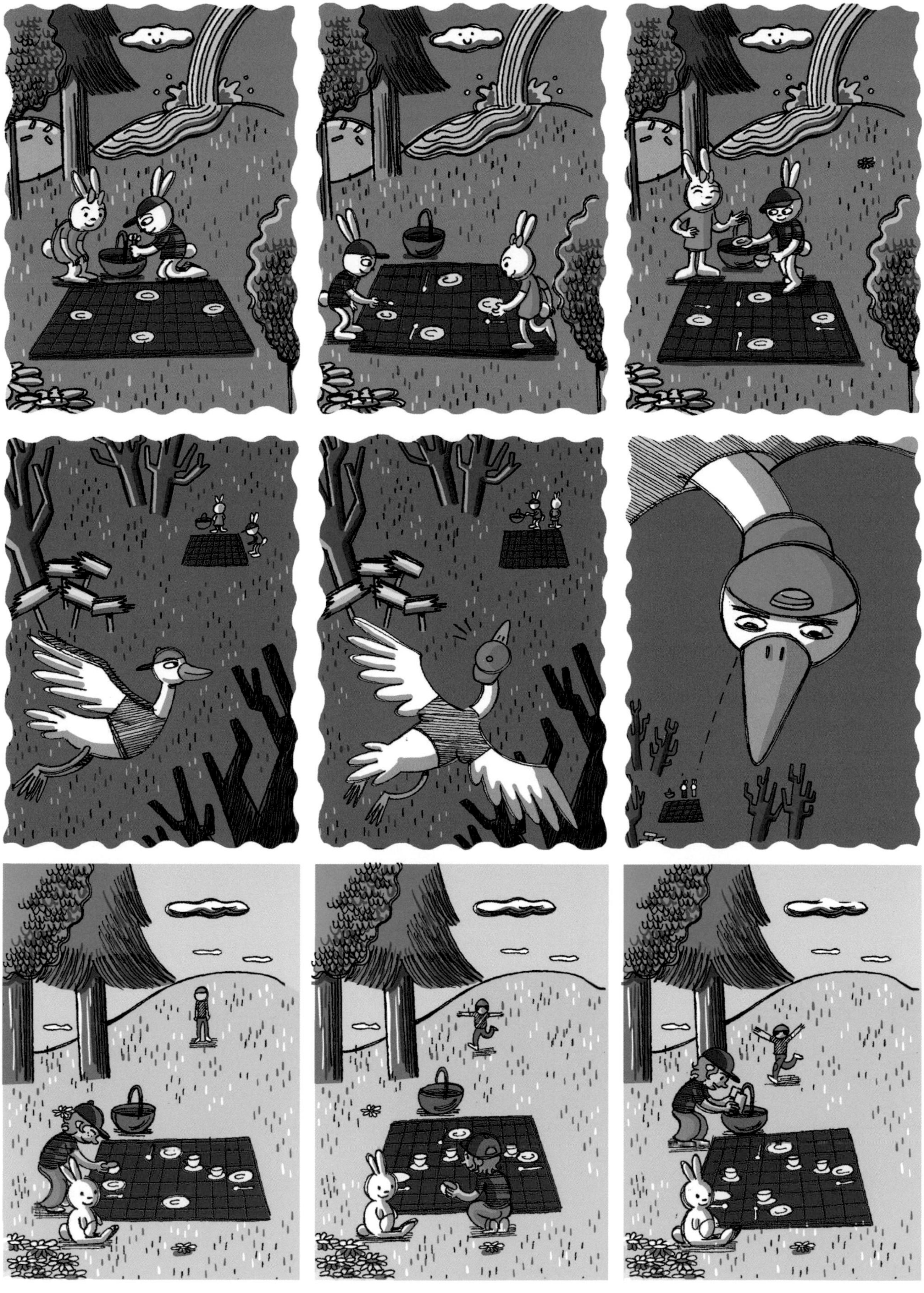

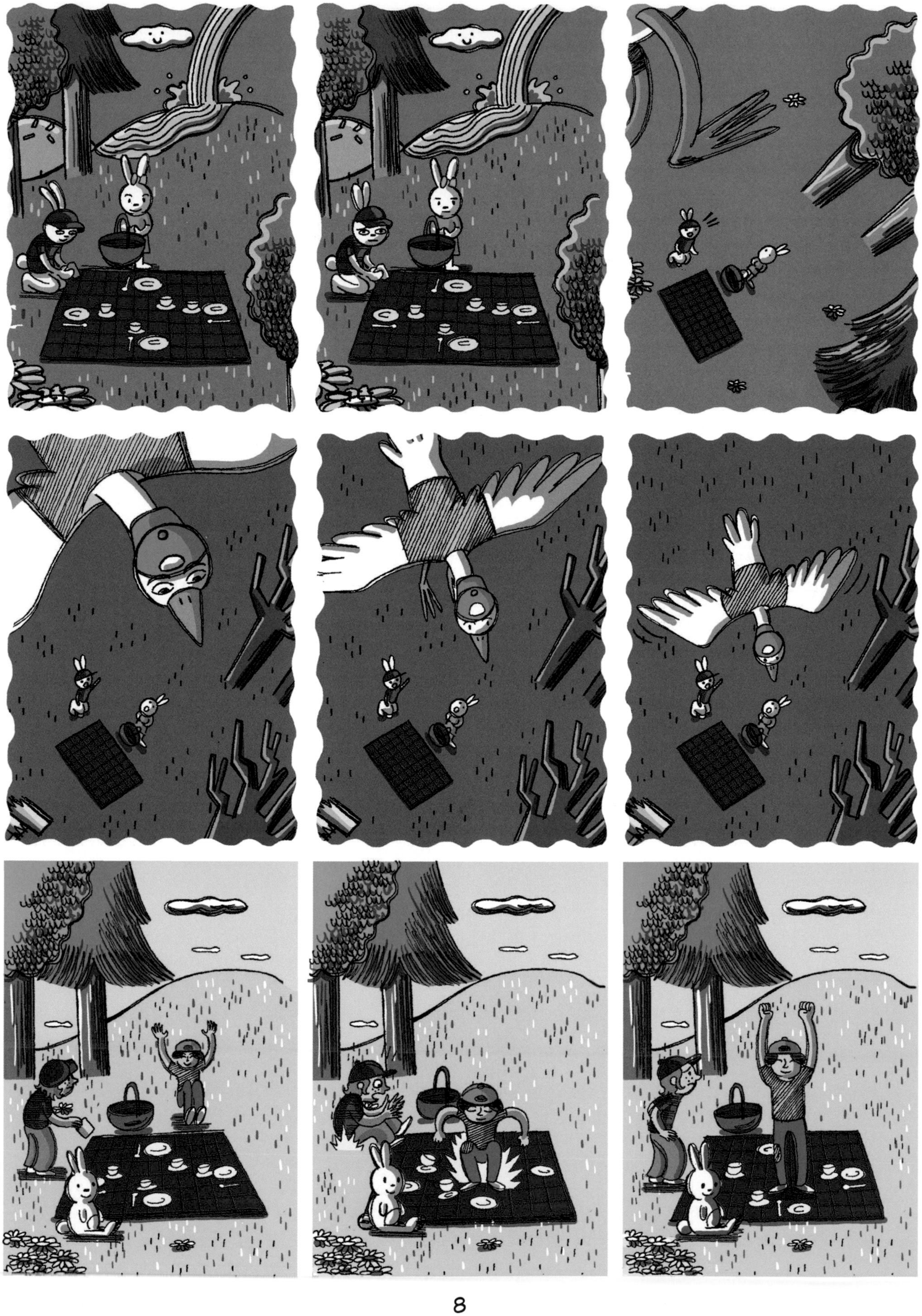

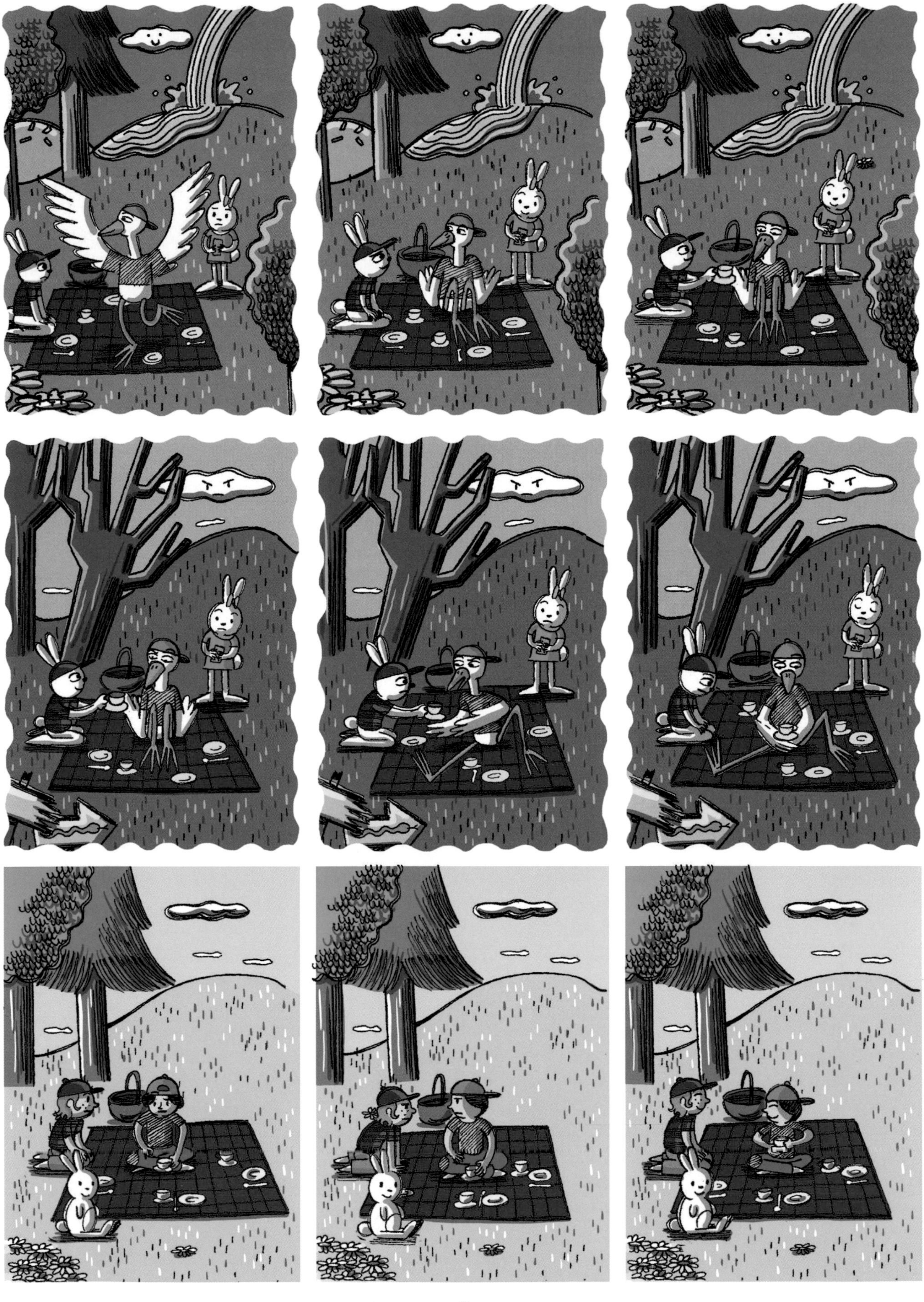

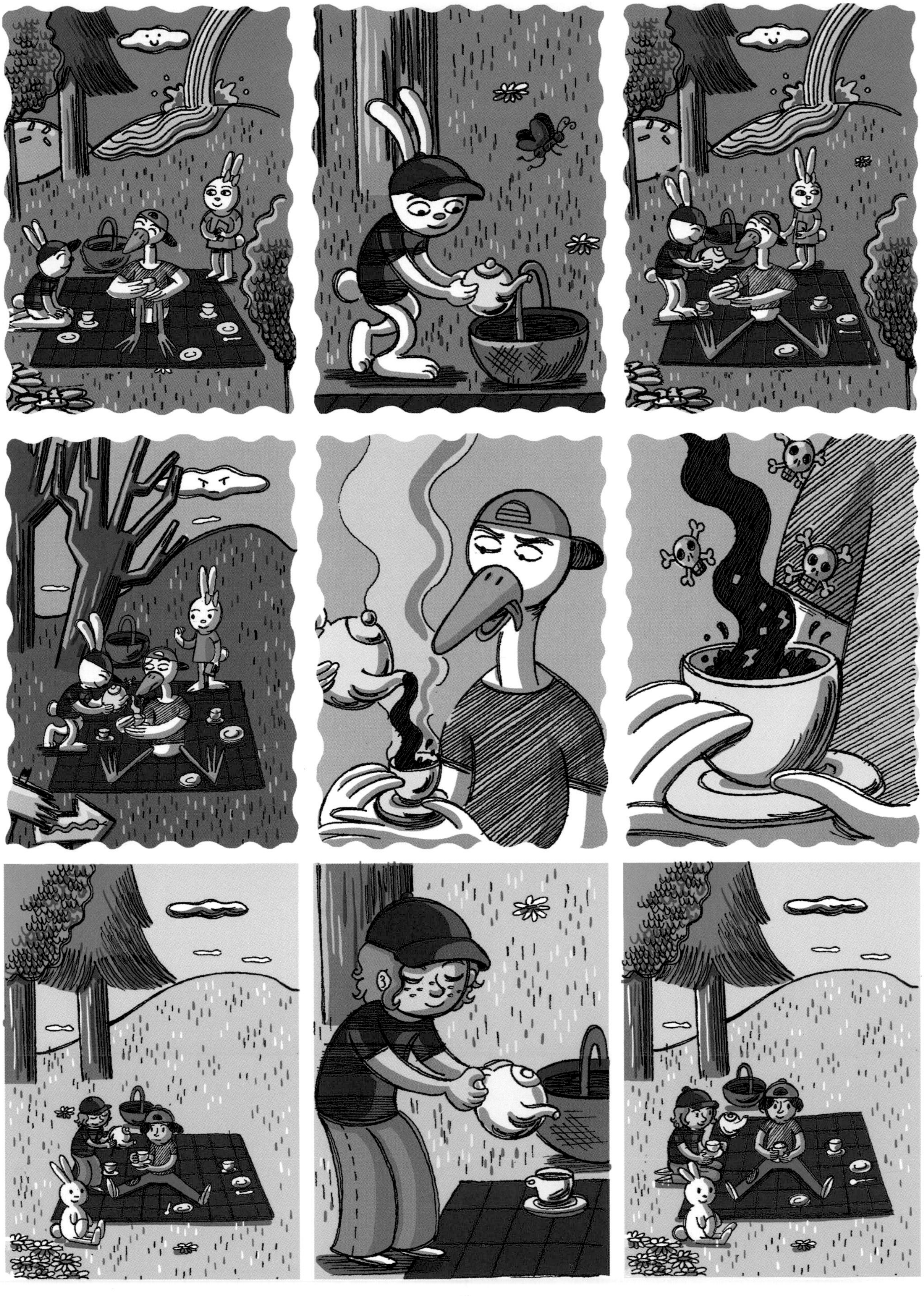

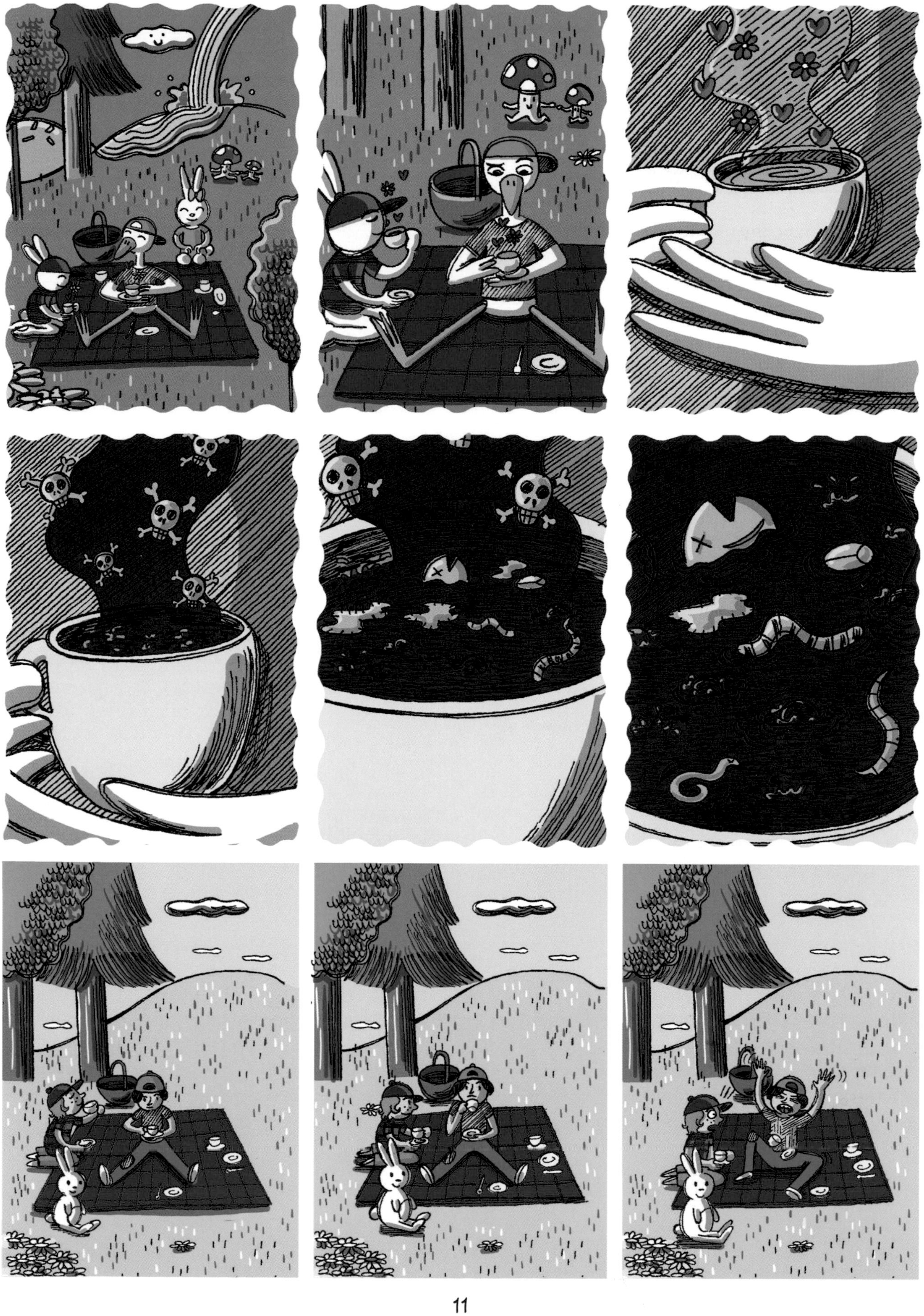

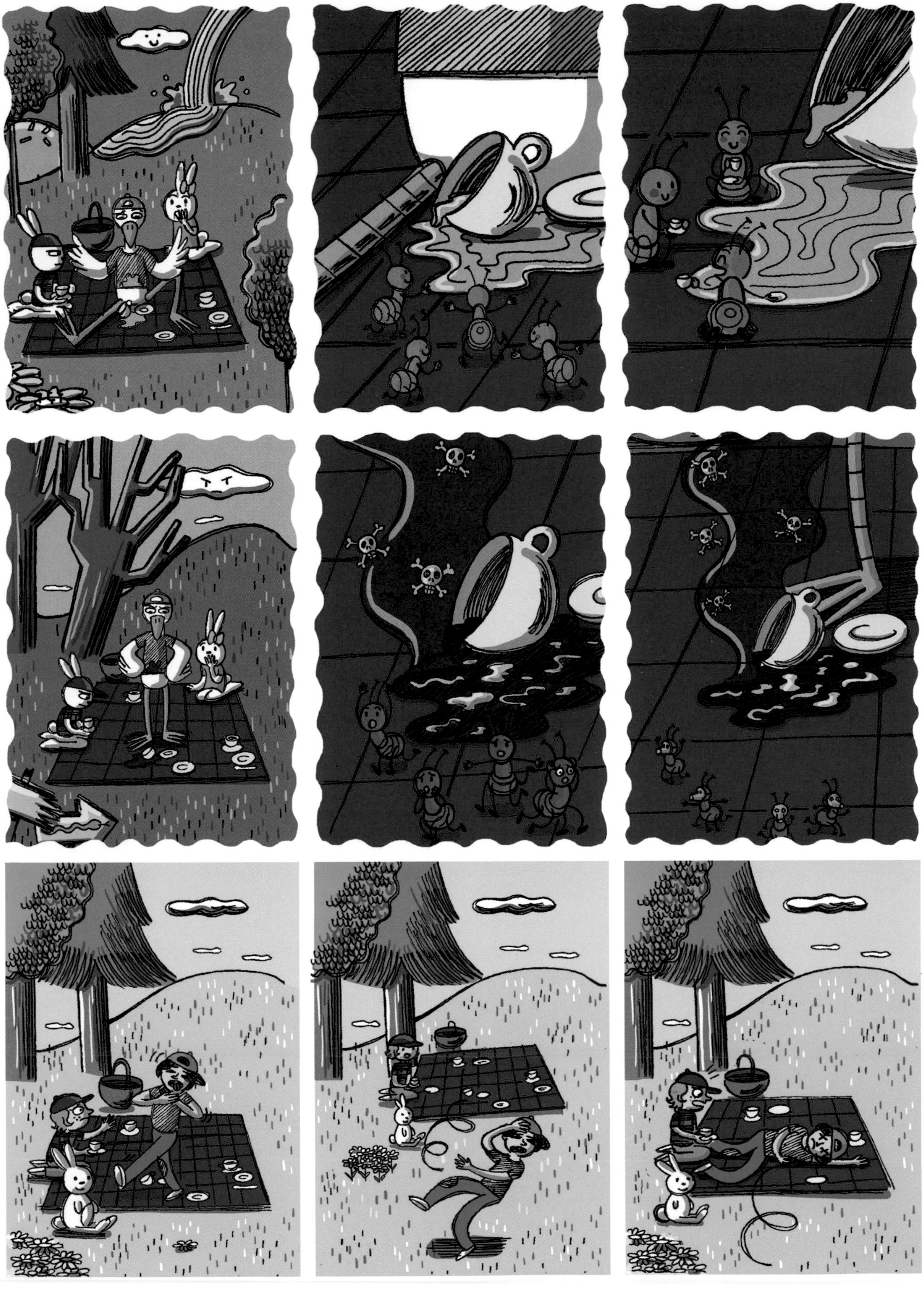

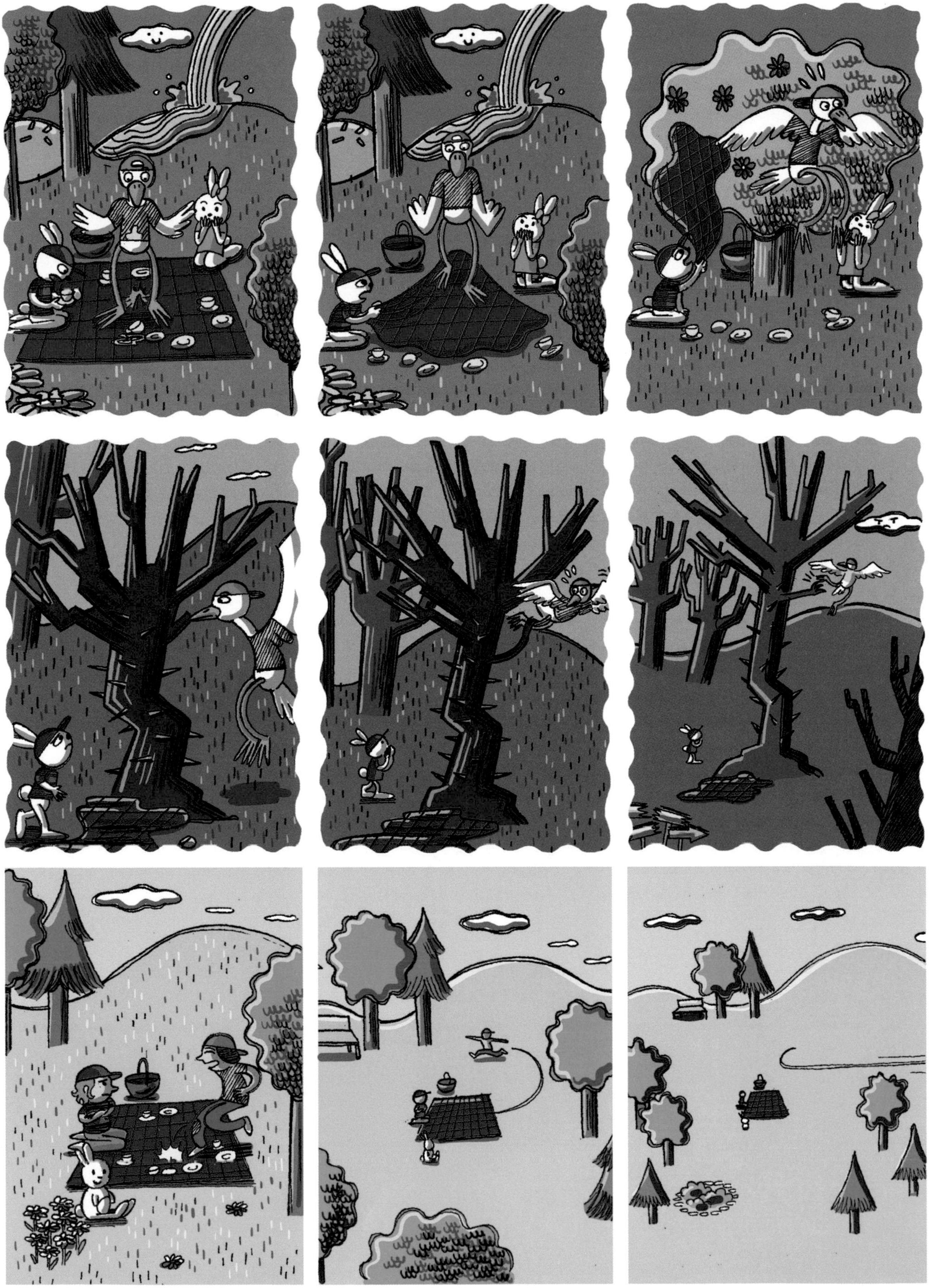

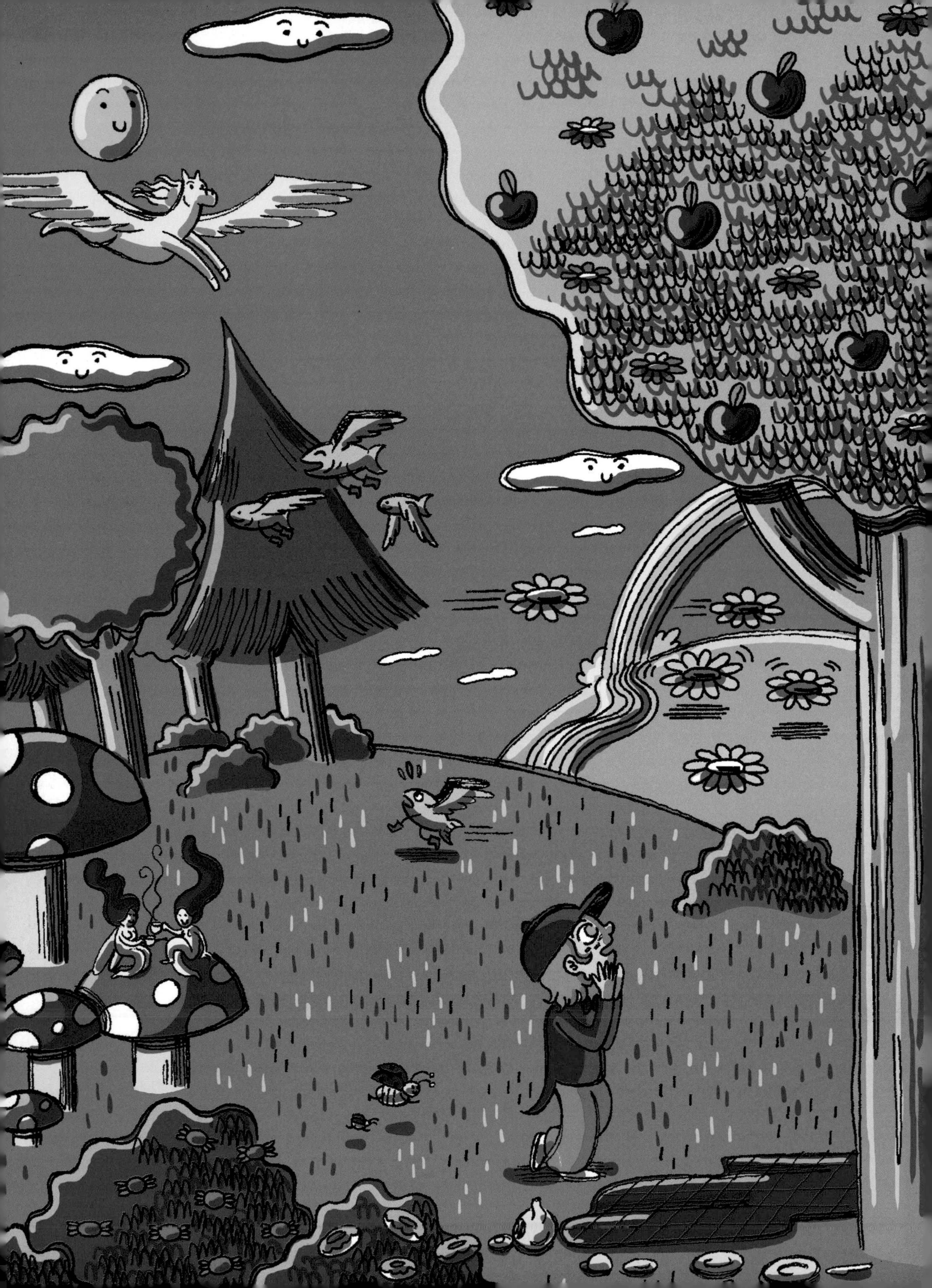

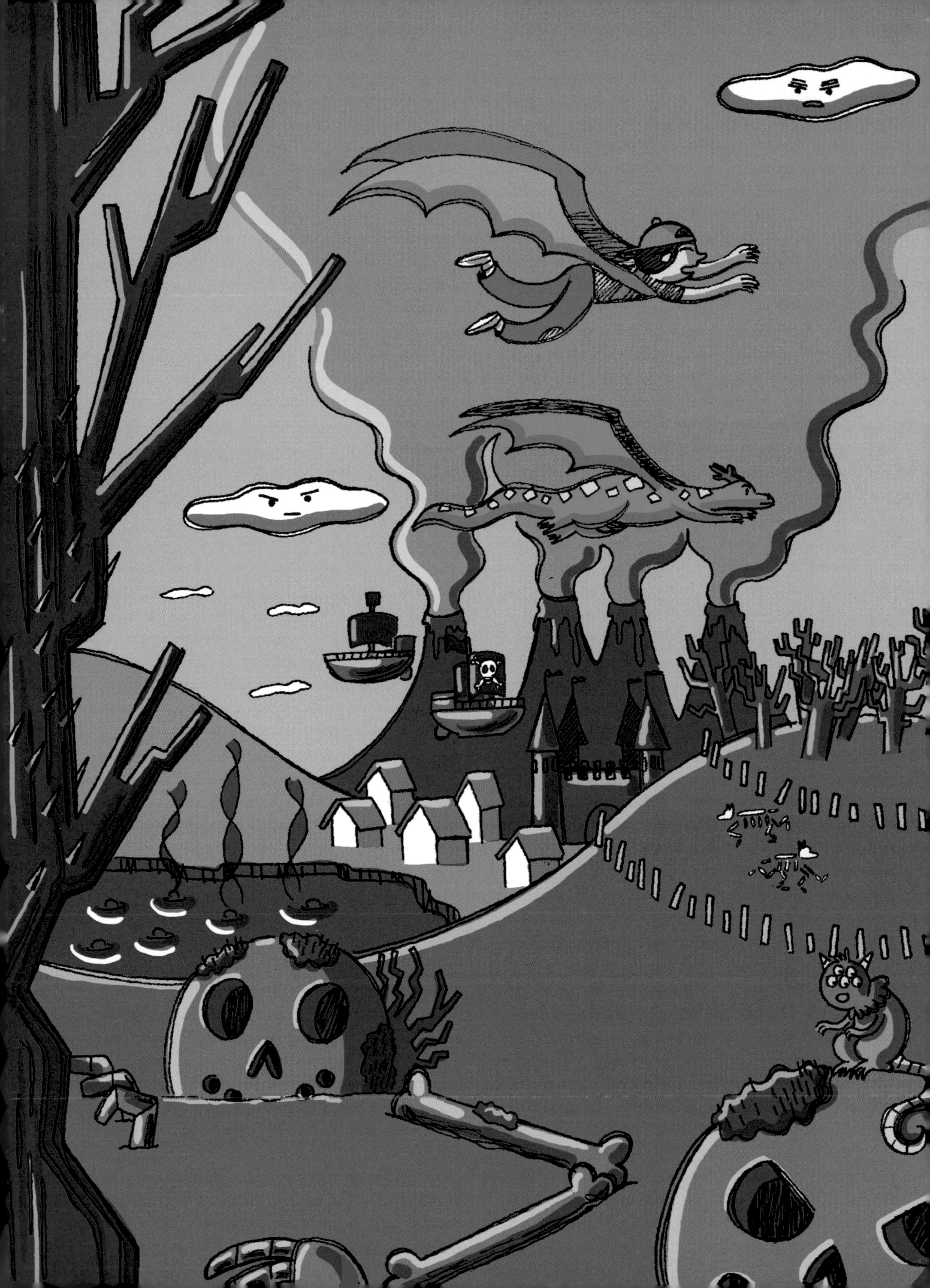

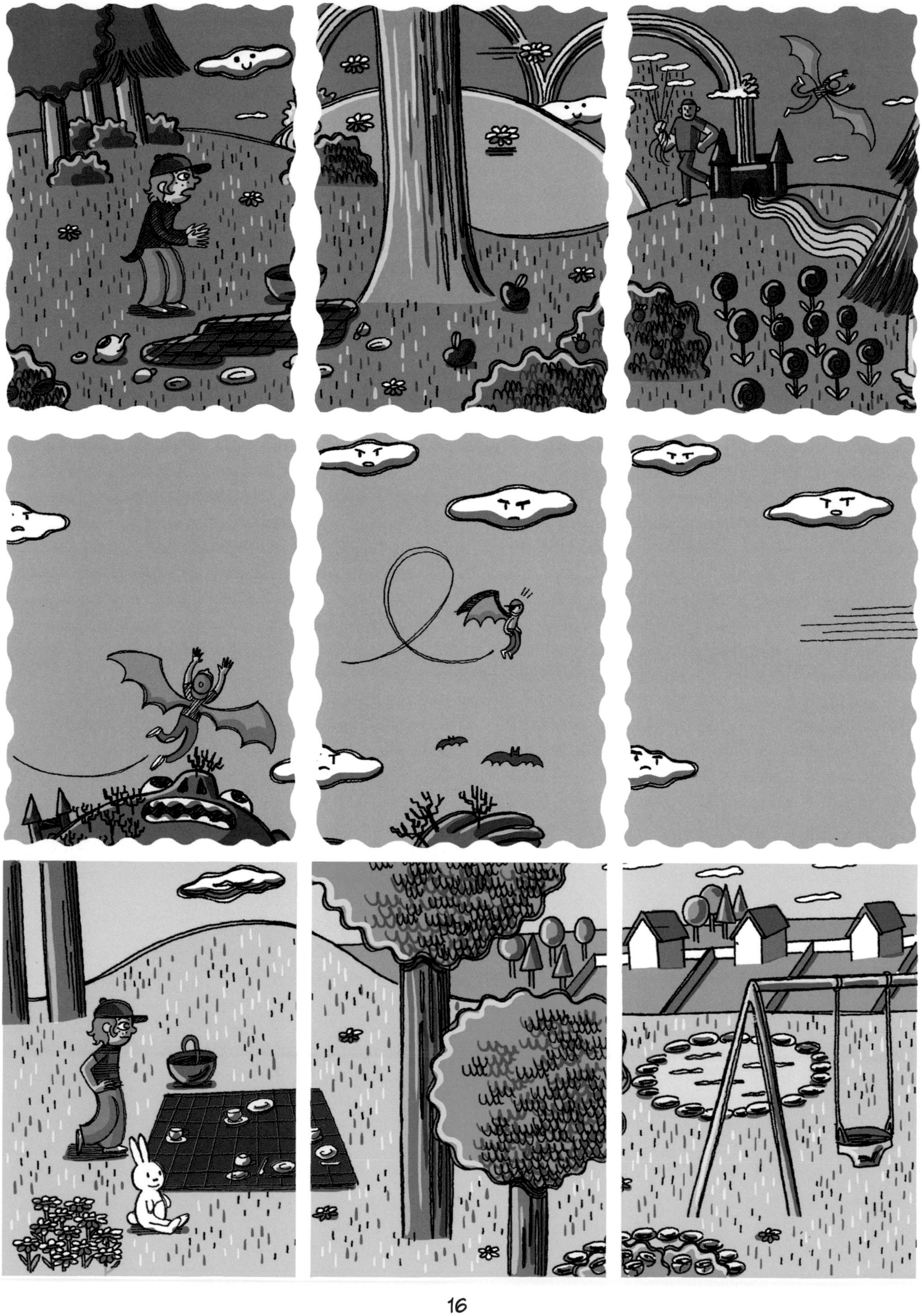

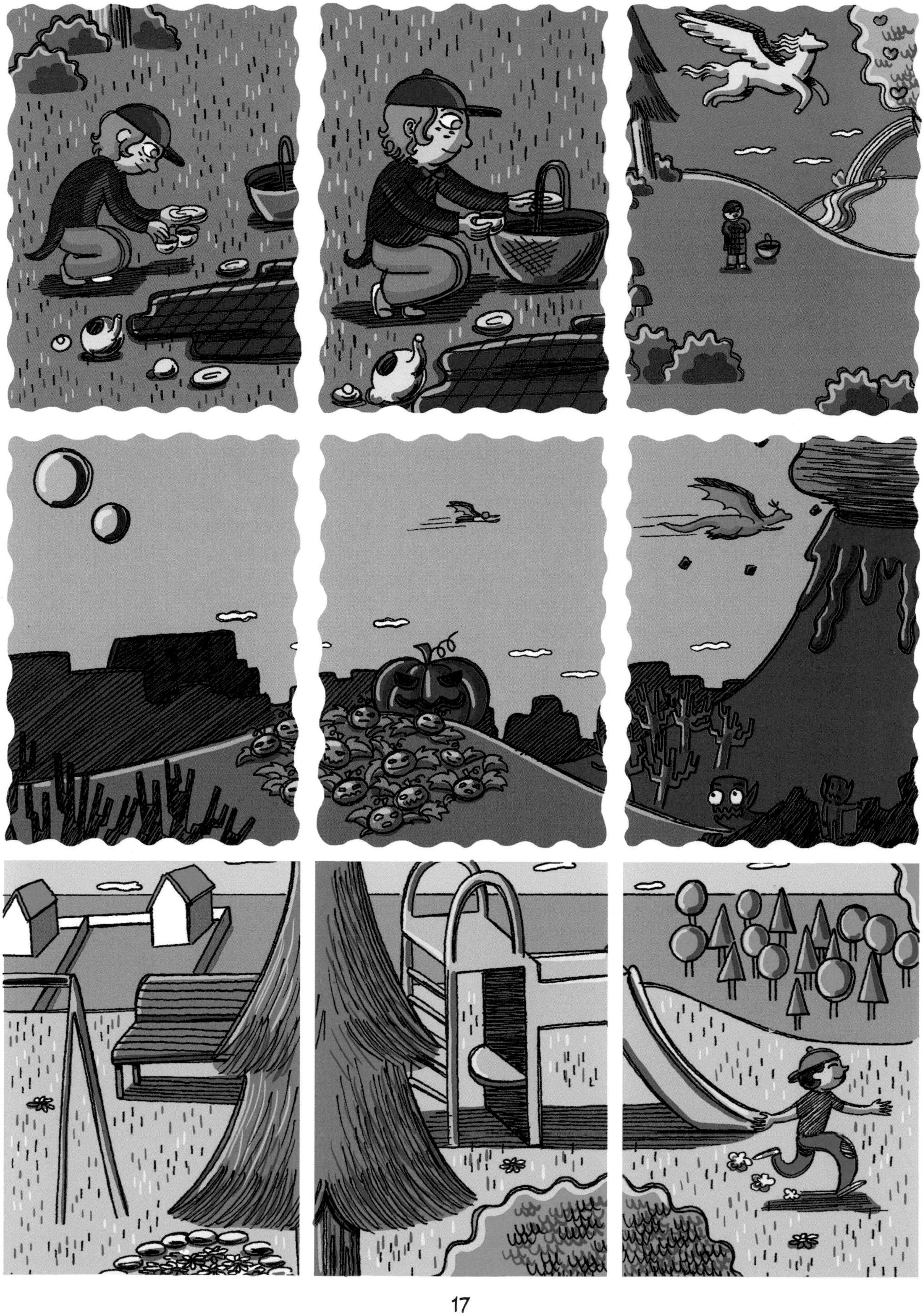

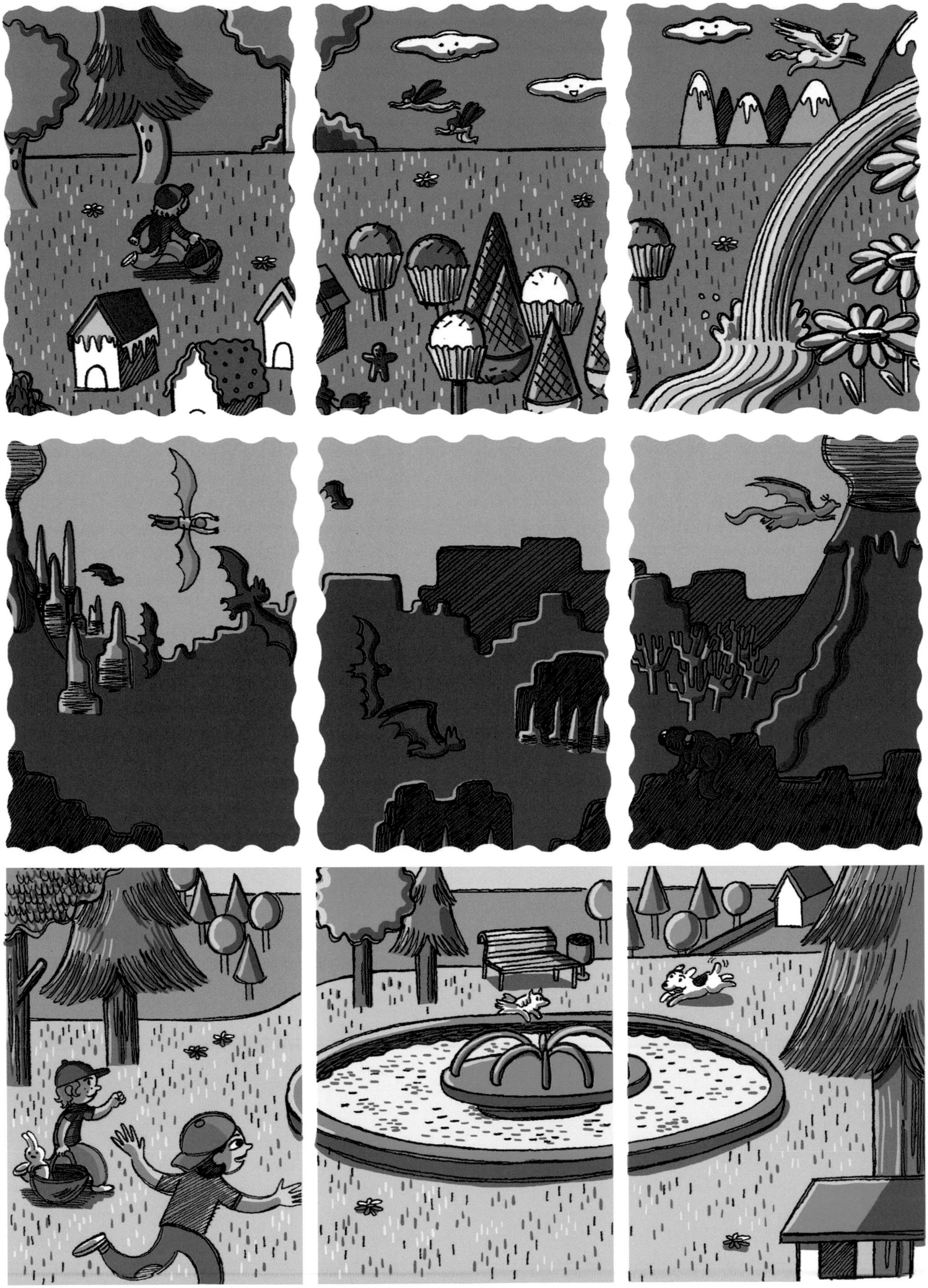

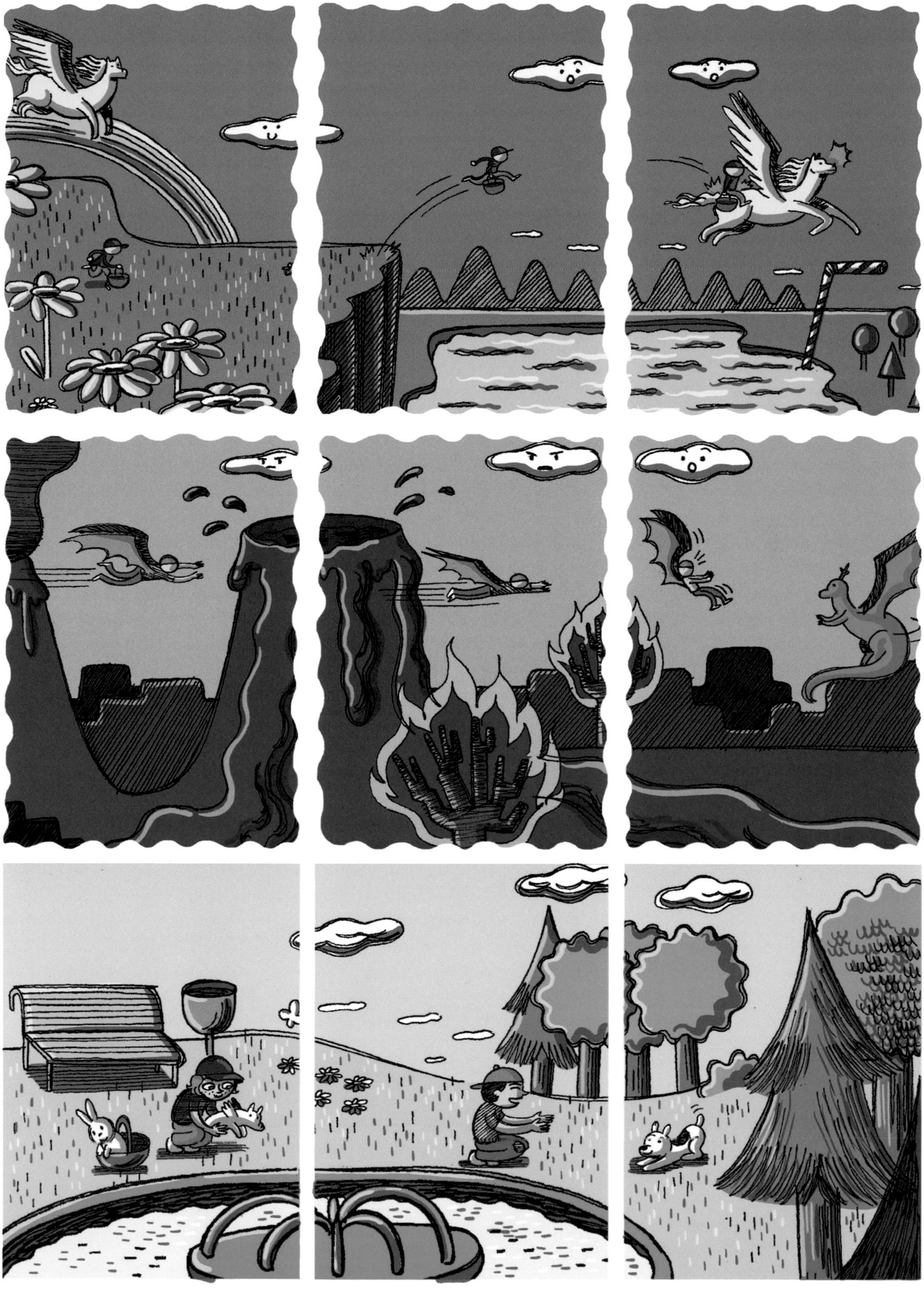

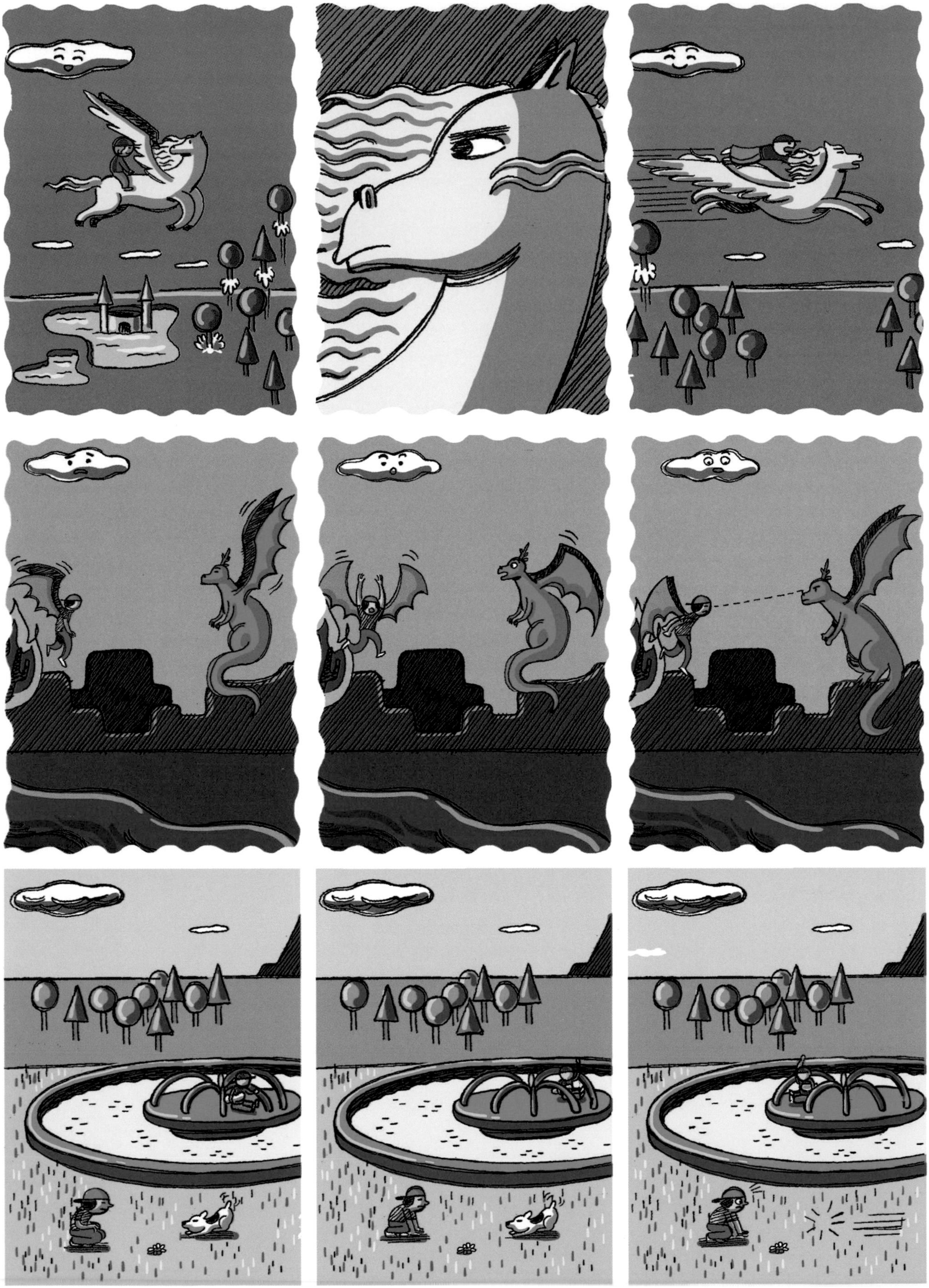

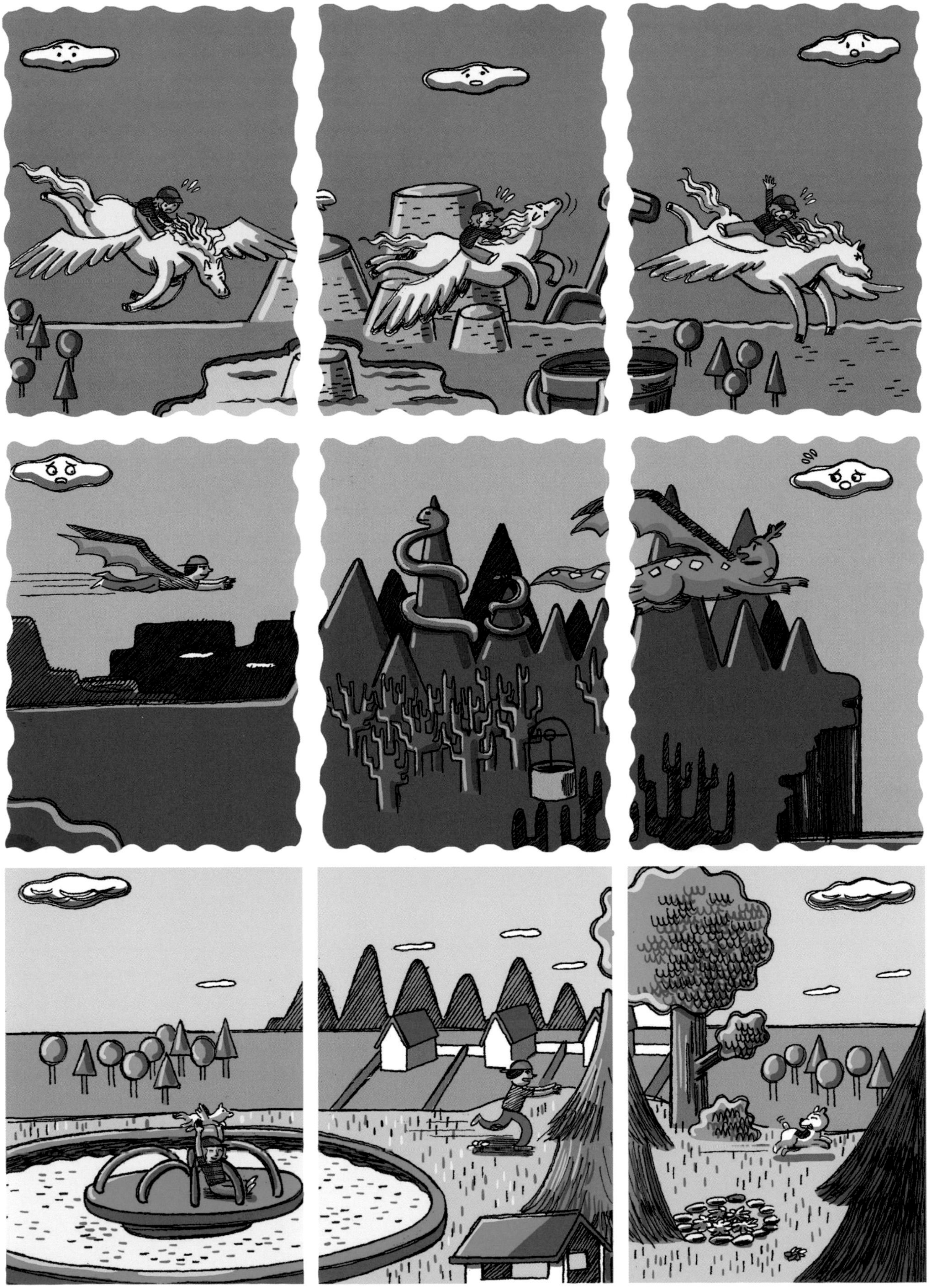

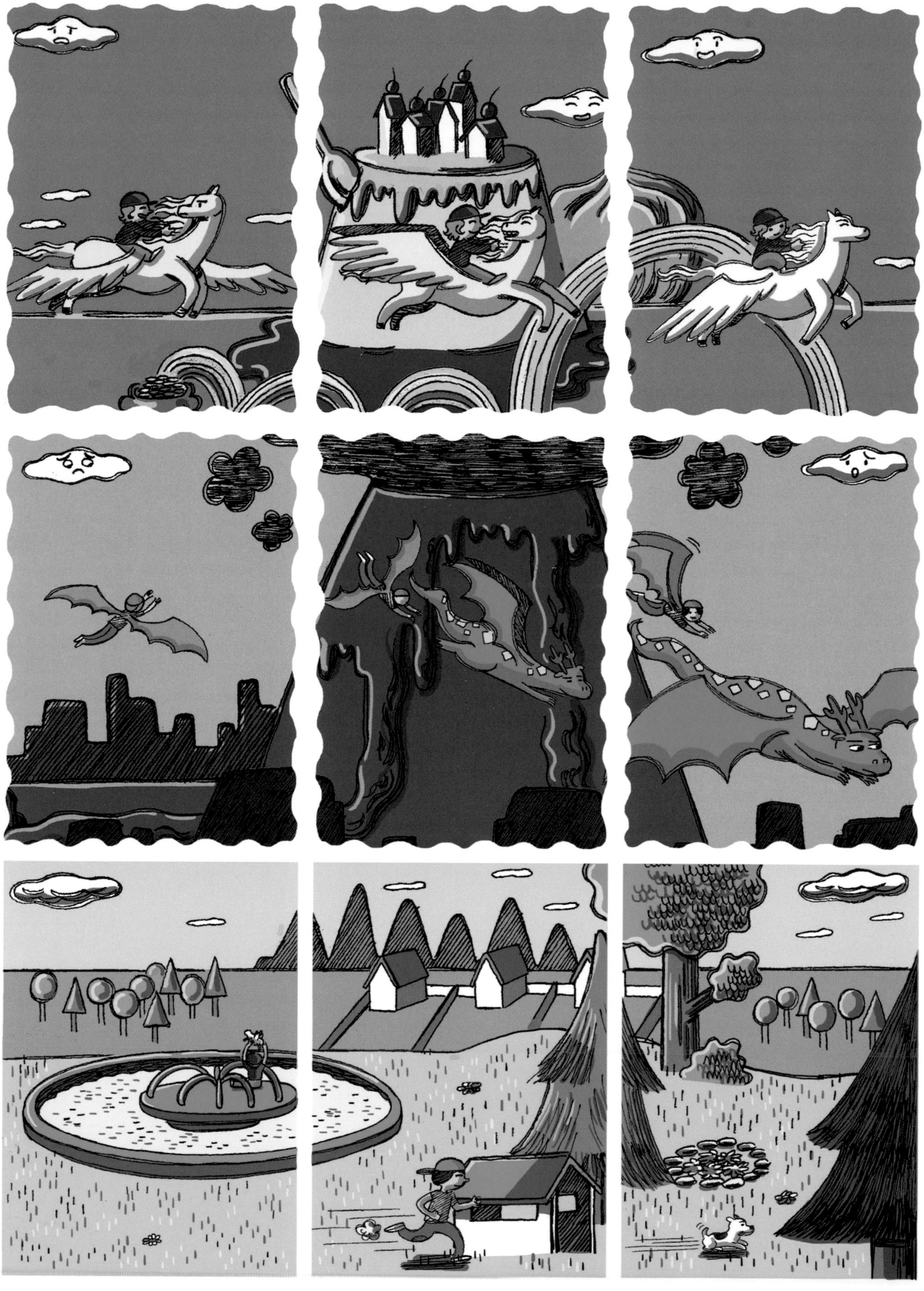

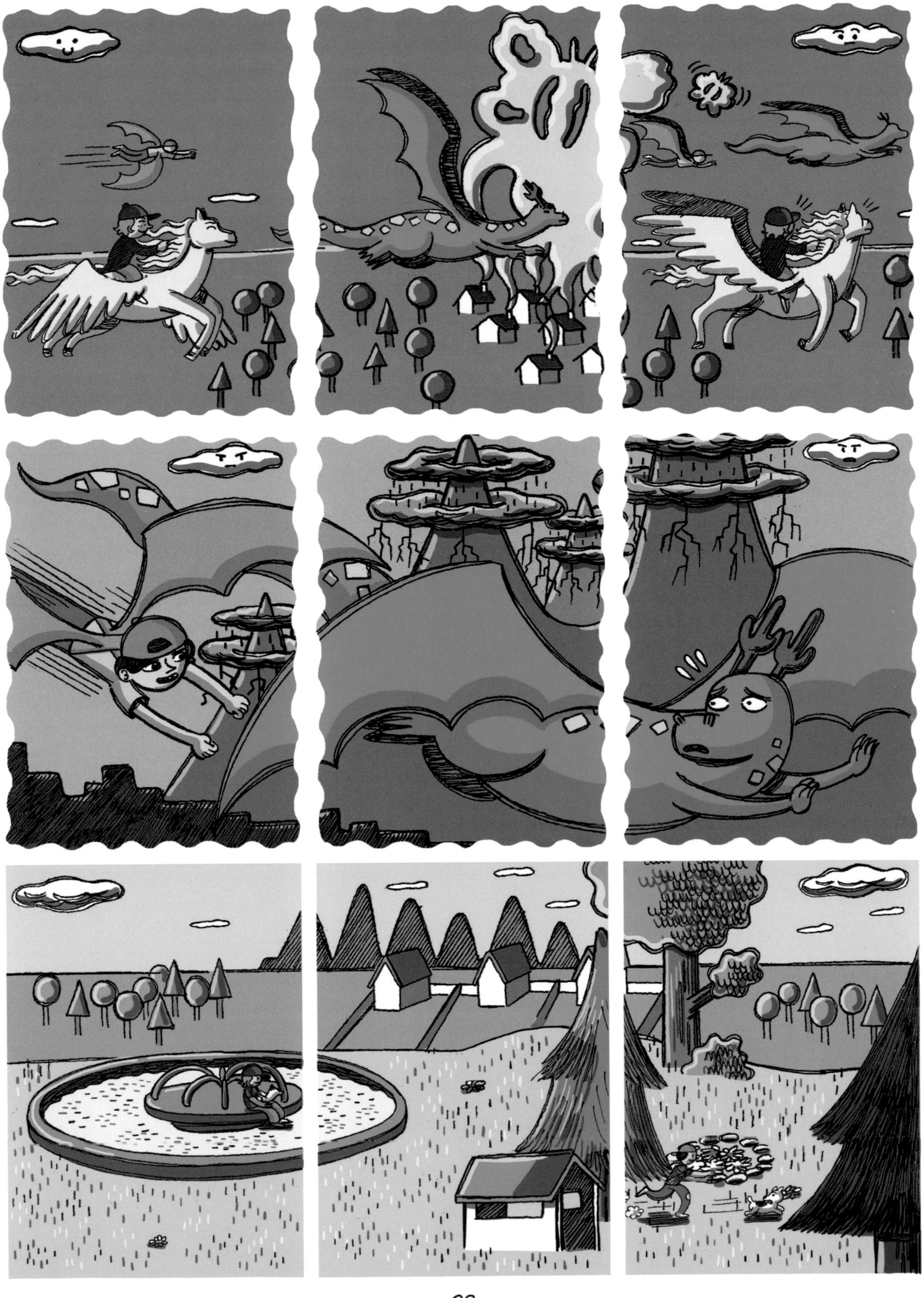

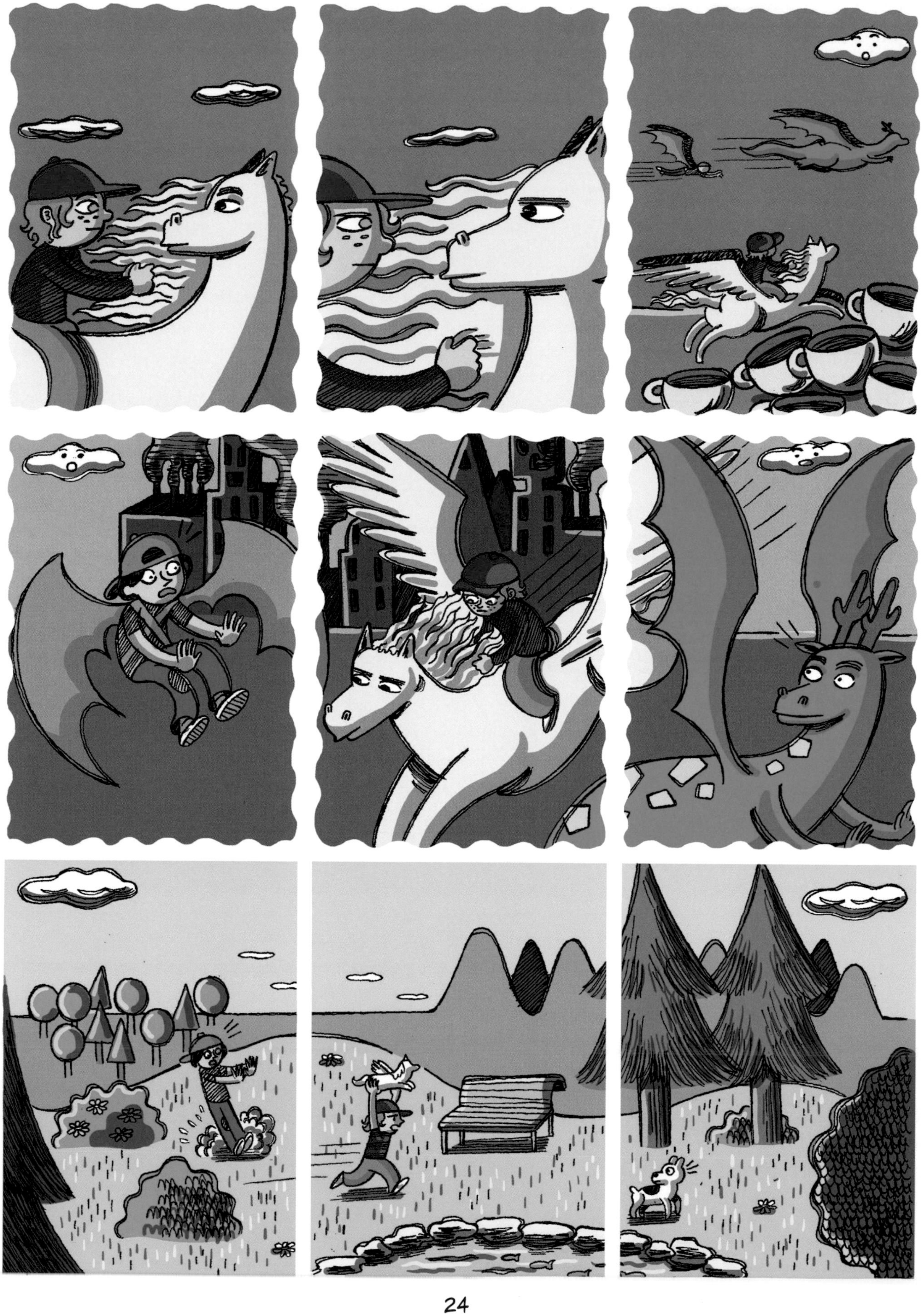

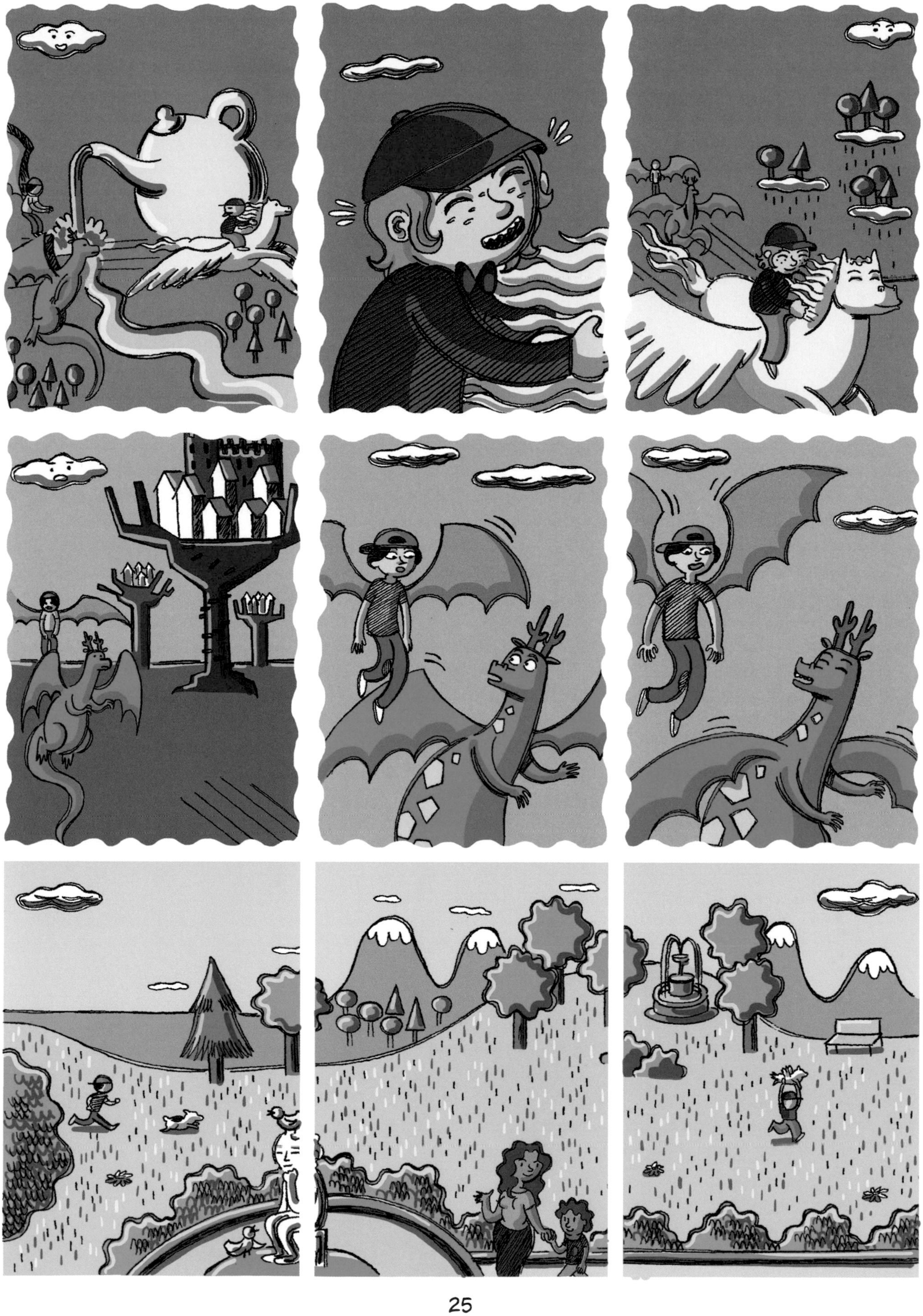

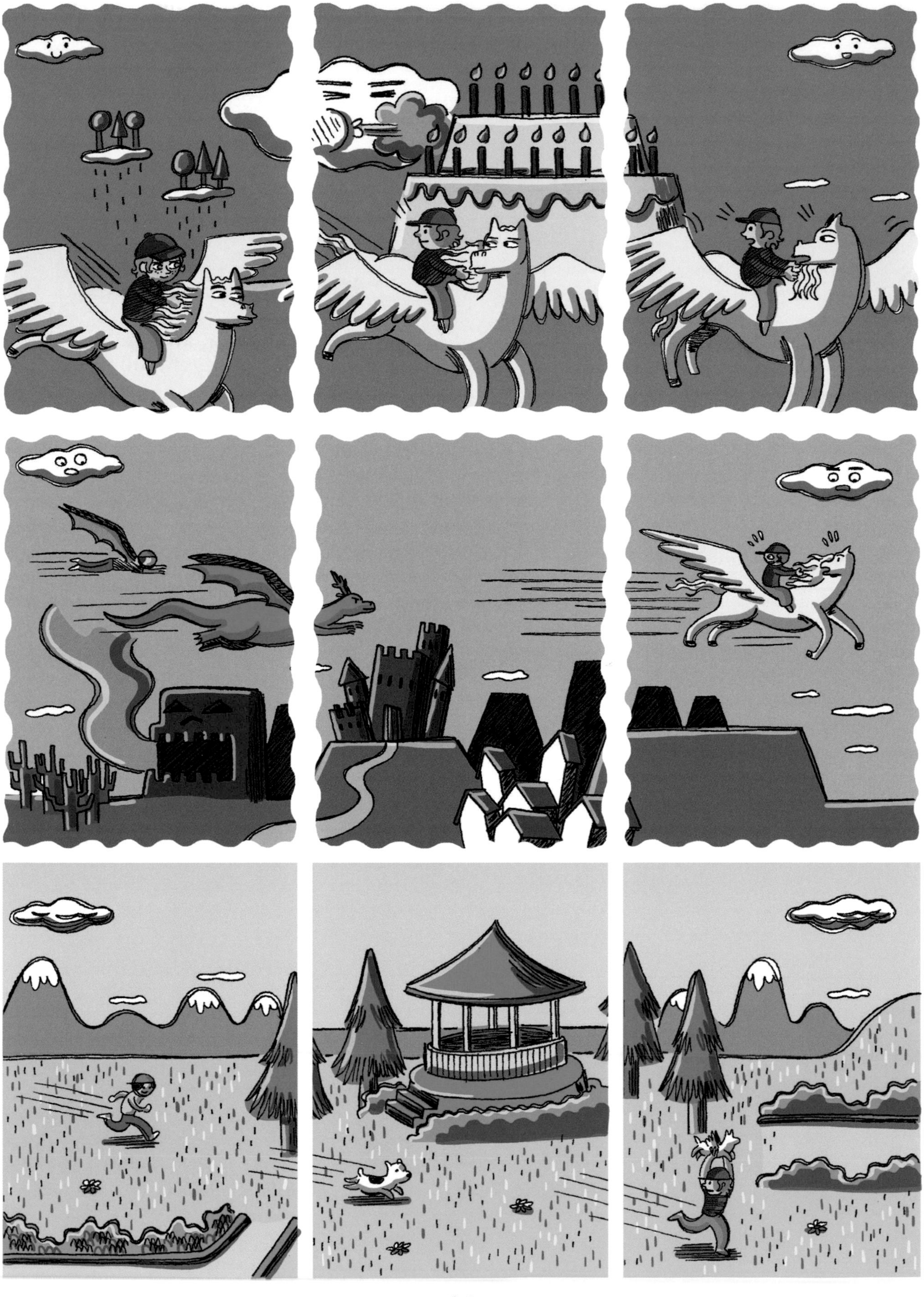

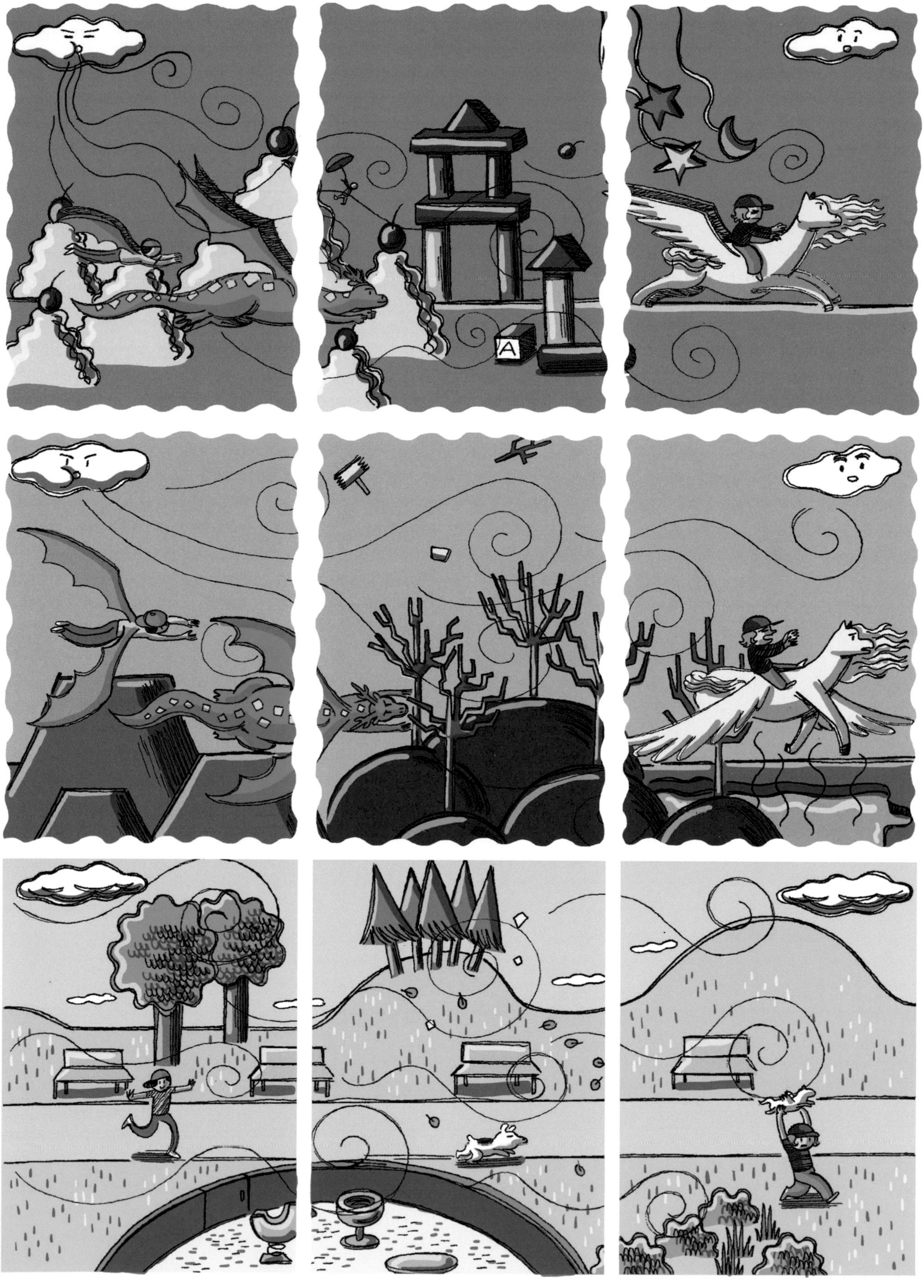
A

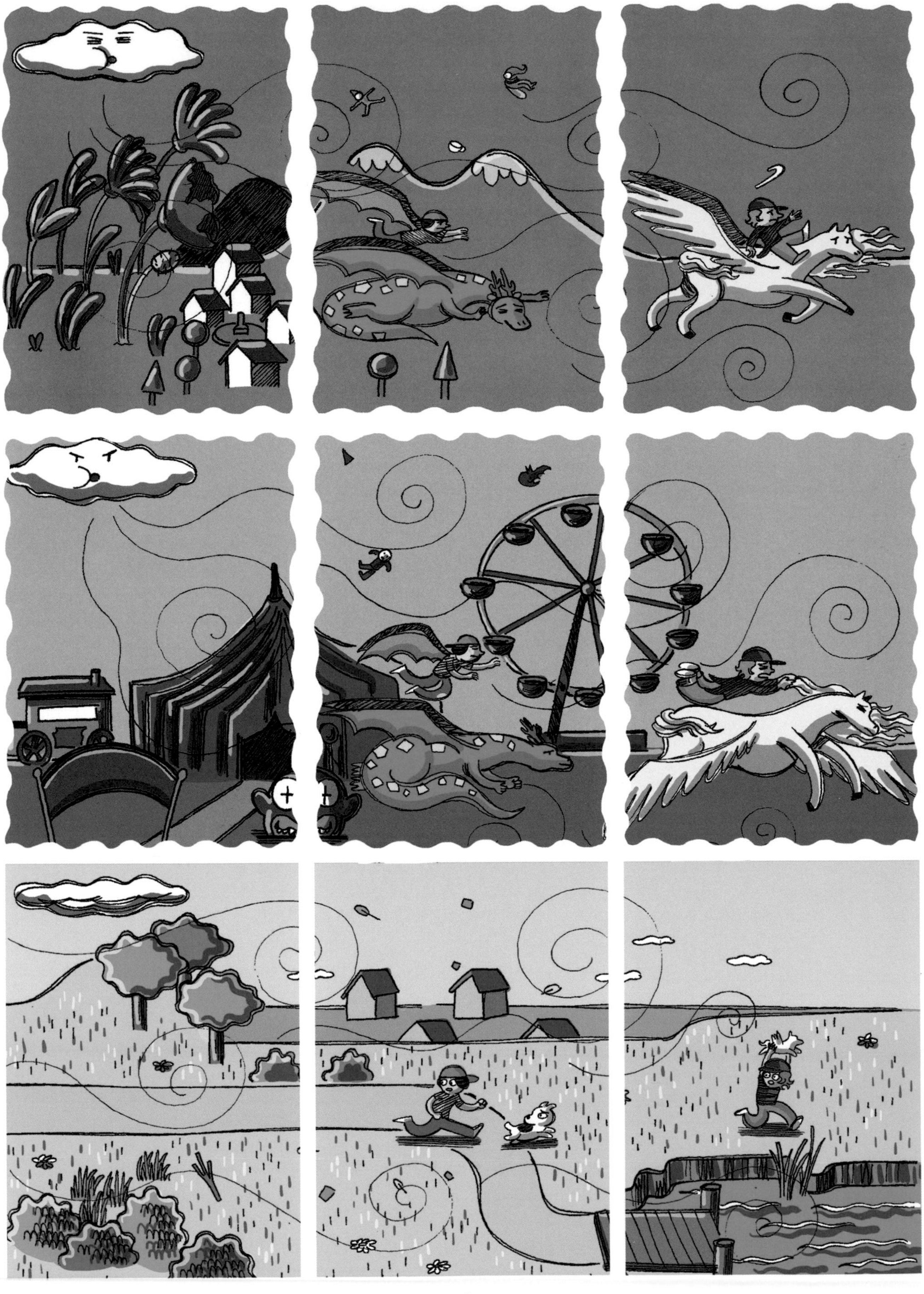

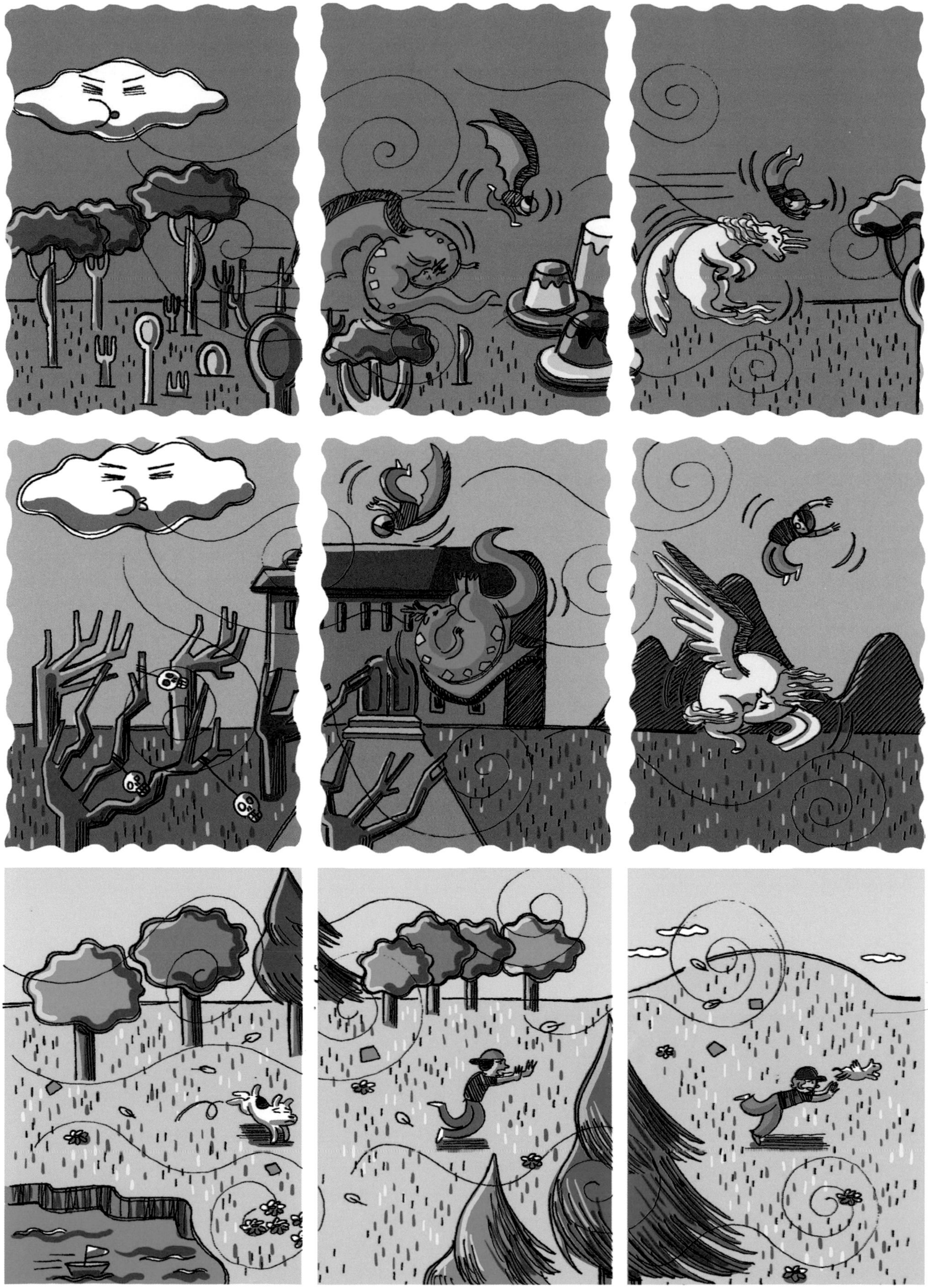

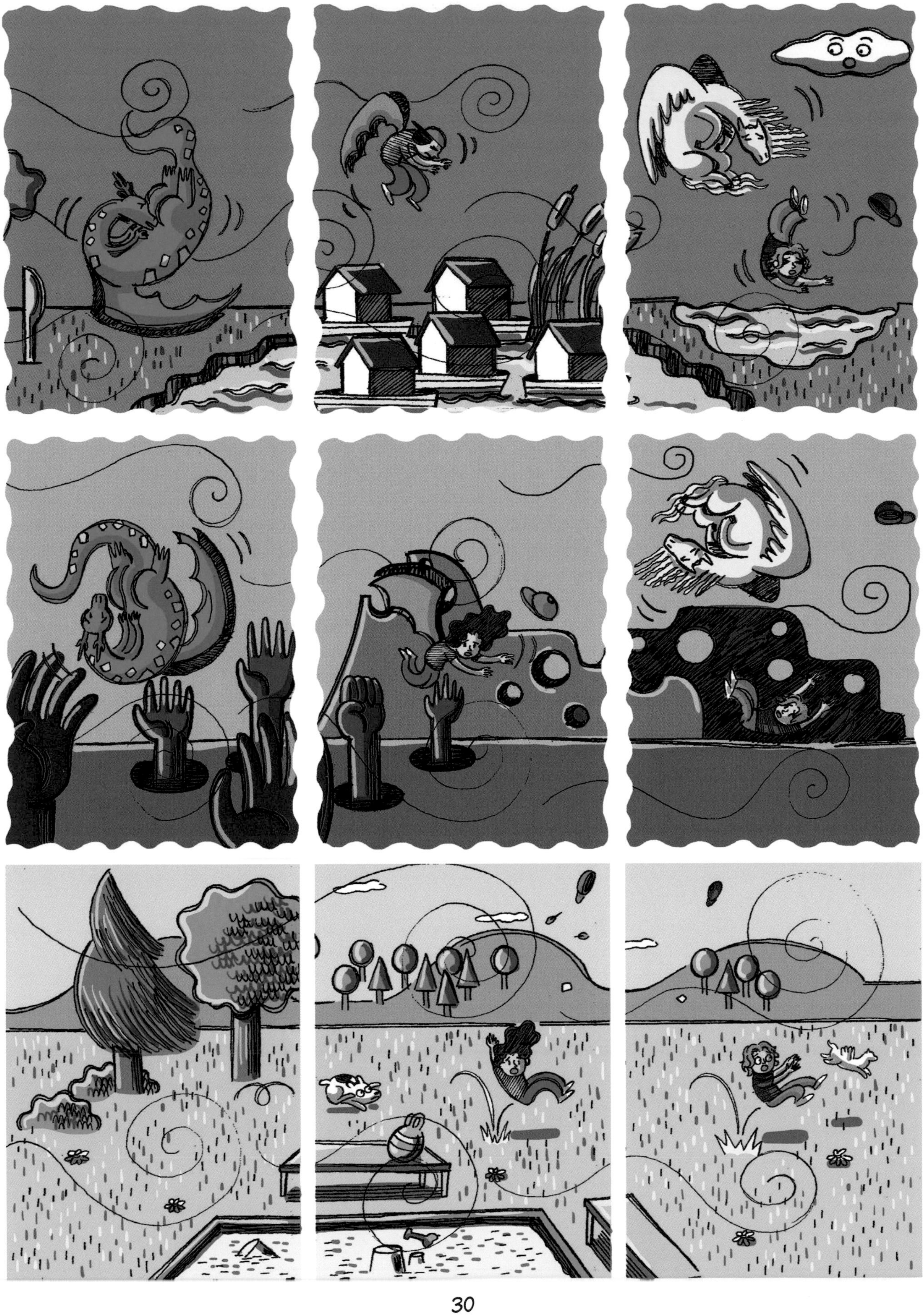

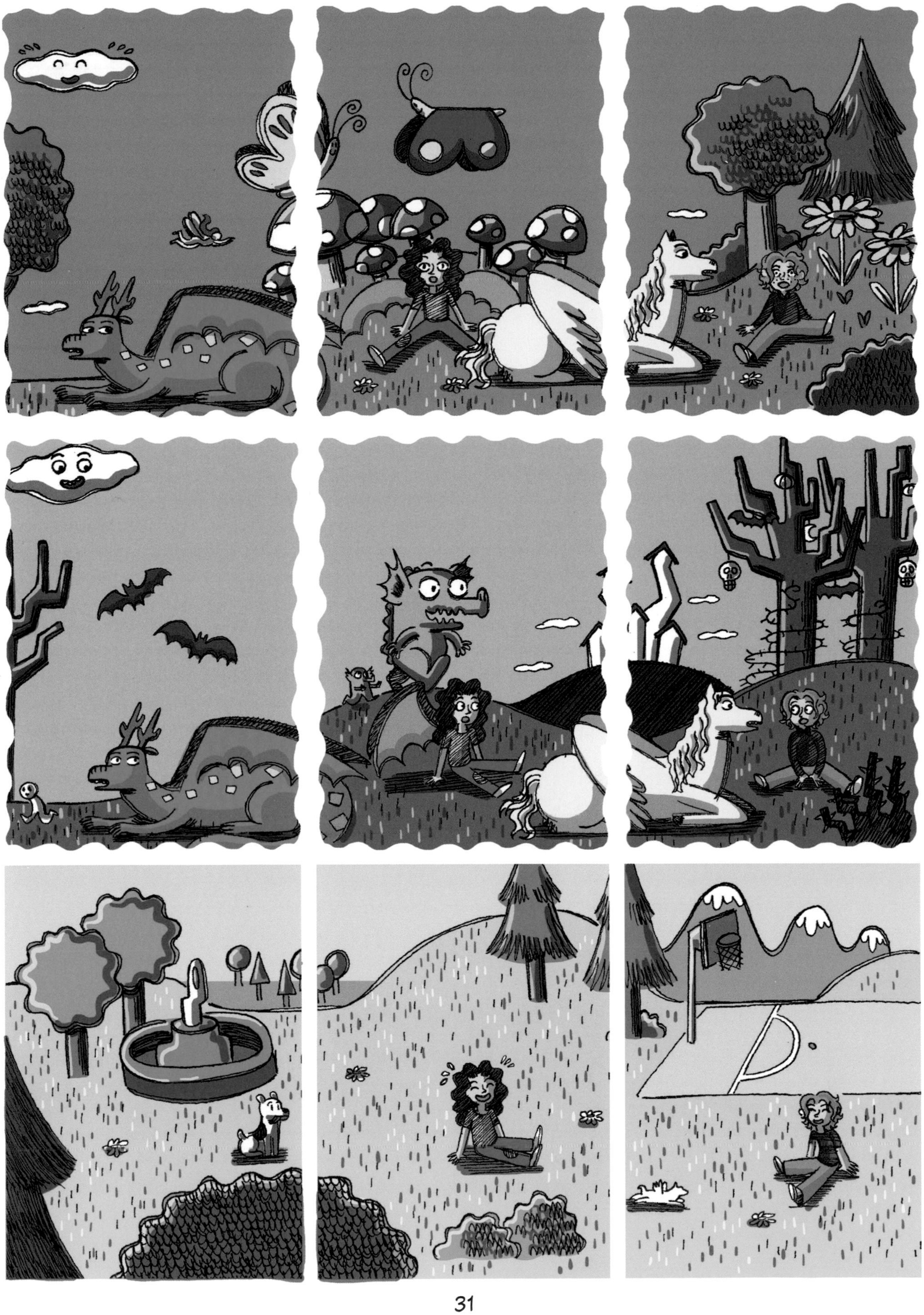

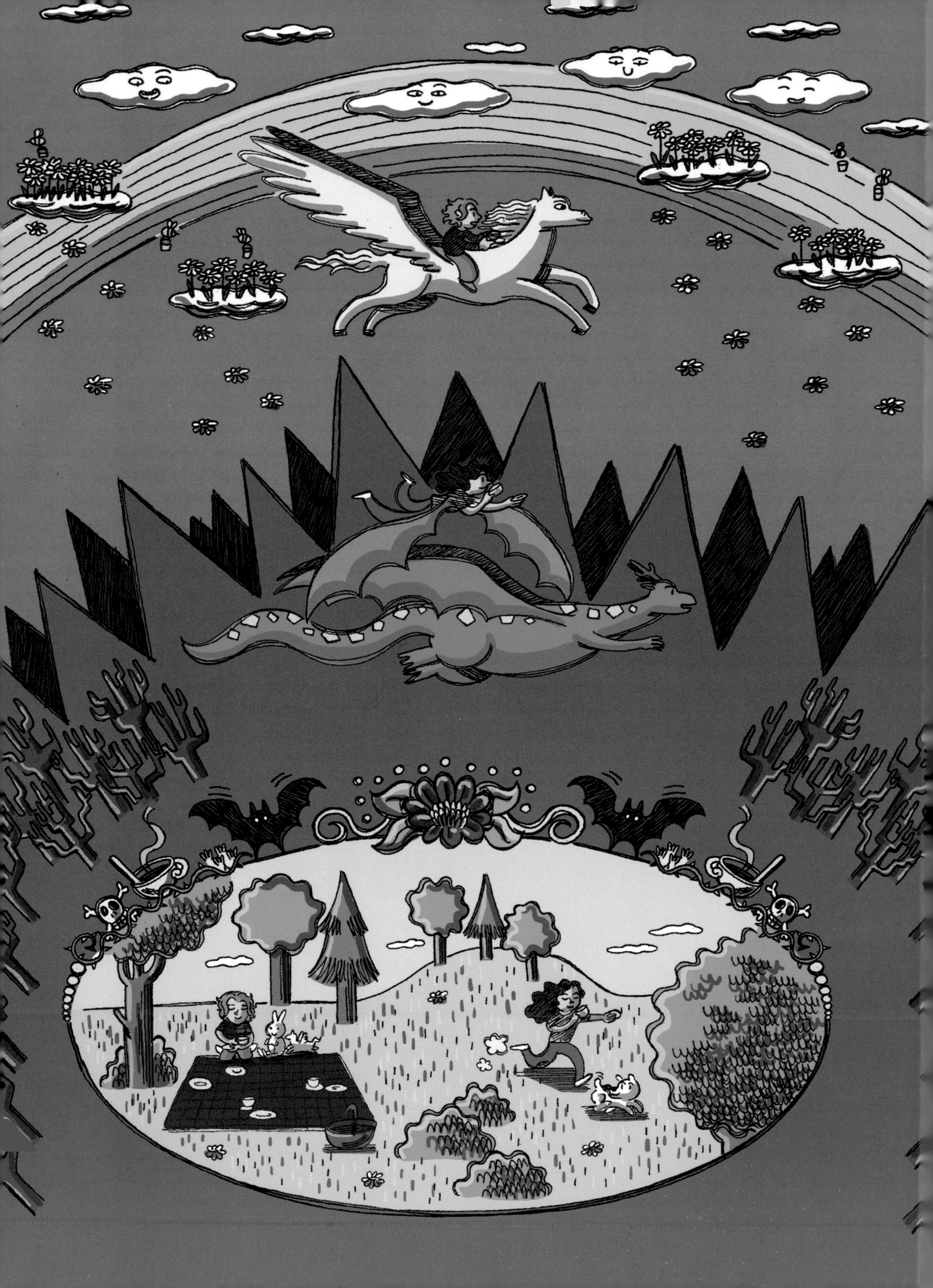

THE END

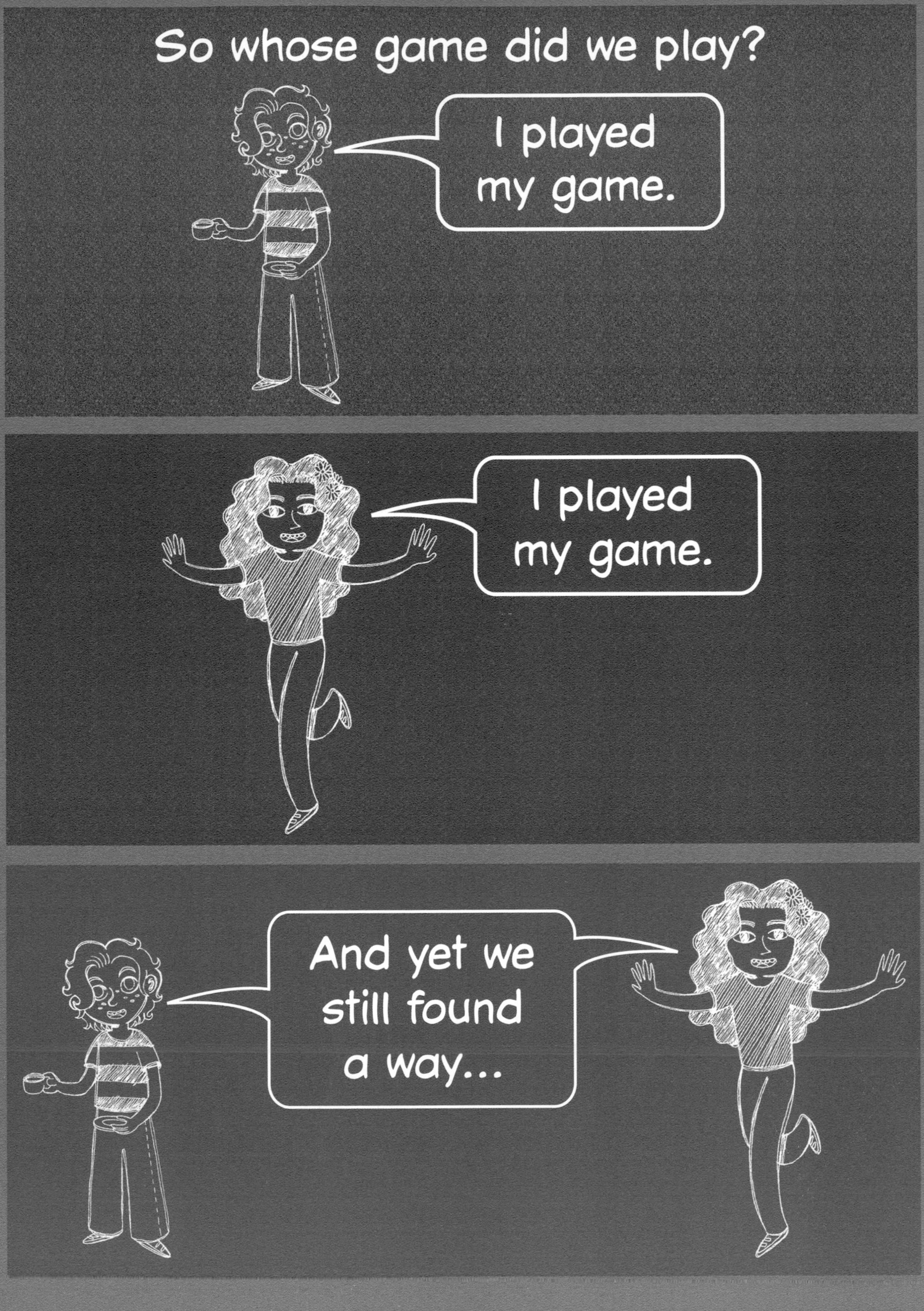
So whose game did we play?
I played my game.
I played my game.
And yet we still found a way...